A Whistle on the Waves

K.M. Woods

ISBN-13: 978-1-7350624-4-0

Cover design by: Levi Hood and Elma Sue Hood
Edited by John McKnight
Library of Congress Control Number: 2018675309
Printed in the United States of America

This novel is dedicated to Coach Donald, Elma Sue, and Levi Hood, three of the dearest friends I know.

Preface

I've found in my limited time on earth that a creative or artistic idea rarely ever begins as something beautiful. Maybe that is my subjective experience, but usually, when I encounter an idea, it strikes wildly, with hints of absurdity, and can even grow chaotic, something far from exalting the human mind or spirit. The mind tends to overdramatize an idea, and usually, it takes diving headfirst into one to discover how riddled with problems it is. It's at this juncture of this discovery where you learn if an idea is even capable of potential beauty because, despite the rather spacey voice in your head that tells you every idea is going to be some wonderful, groundbreaking masterpiece, the truth is that some ideas are just bad.

A Whistle on the Waves, as an idea, never met that juncture. Back when the idea struck, this was odd to me. I struggled, and continue, turning my first novel idea, *The Ginger Who Snapped*, into a reasonable narrative, much less a good one. Even after seven years since beginning it, I'm still battling to put that novel into words (Why its has been spared of the literary grave, who knows?) I probably couldn't count, if I took the time to try, just how many ideas have died horrible deaths after jotting some notes, character webs, or journals. But from the moment the story in *A Whistle on the Waves* appeared like magic, I knew instantly it was one of inherent beauty.

Being able to capture that beauty with the pen was another battle entirely.

Back in that time, I lived a life of constant agitation, concealing (though not quietly) a dying urge to break away from my hometown. I was living in New Orleans, driving a pedicab in the French Quarter for money, and acting in local theatre productions. I'd dropped out of college, my attitude sucked, and I arrogantly thought I'd seen and experienced everything Louisiana had to offer. Then one morning, cruising down I-10 in my Mazda B-series truck to a Saturday morning rehearsal, the host of an NPR program introduced a folk band. I regretfully forget their name, however, I didn't forget the song they played. *The Lakes of Ponchartrain*.

Who, I wondered, would write a song about that dirty-ass lake, Lake Ponchartrain?'

Three minutes later, as the studio audience broke into slow applause, I fought to bottle in the emotion the song had evoked. For those of you who've never heard the lyrics, the song tells a vague, but heartbreaking story about a man wandering, penniless and friendless, in the springtime, '*bidding New Orleans adieu*'. On the banks of Lake Pontchartrain, he meets a beautiful creole woman, who takes him into her cottage, shows him true kindness, and, after a short time, he falls in love with her. Take my word for it that this brief description does not bring the song justice in any stretch of the imagination, but from that moment, I knew a novel might. I saw an angry soldier, bitter, grieving, blaming the world for his problems. I saw him navigating through a much older New Orleans, recently taken by the Union. And after some moderate research and discovery of the Celtic origins of *The Lakes of Pontchartrain*, I saw that my soldier's Irish heritage likely explained why *the strangers there were no friends to him*.

Not too long after this touching moment in my car, I moved to New York and wrote the first draft of what was then titled *By the Lakes*. I can't remember exactly when the whistle came into play, but I know it was inspired by the flute solo after the chorus in Paul Brady's version of the song. I'd listened to this version well over a hundred times. After three years, four drafts, two full edits, and more automated rejection letters than I could pull up in my email's past messages, here, I offer you that novel I saw in my head on that frustrated Saturday morning. While I can't know for certain if I was capable of capturing the beauty or true heart of *The Lakes of Pontchartrain*, the experience of writing this surely fed my life some much-needed satisfaction and soulful fulfillment. Such was the beauty of the experience. For that and that alone, I have no regrets in writing it and I hope it feeds you some of the same. Thank you for taking the time to read it.

A Whistle on the Waves

Part One

Shane

One

When we were young, it was clear how much the whistle annoyed me. Shane would slip it out of his pocket, and I'd see the dull shimmer of faded grey, lusterless metal, and a pit of irritation grew in my gut as I thought, "Why do I have to stop talking for this stupid toy?" Shane noticed my distaste, but that didn't stop him from eeking out the notes into some tune, a semblance of music. At first, any song with a moderately fast rhythm sounded like a squealing rat minutes from death, but over time, he got better. But I never had a lick of appreciation for the whistle or his constant need to play it through the years.

He cared about the damn thing though. He never left it strewn on the floor, or in some dusty cupboard; never abandoned it carelessly. He carried it with him always, tucked neatly in his pocket. He carried it across the ocean, playing it whenever he could, and for him, it was something rich that brought a fulfilling intimacy in his life that I never thought to understand. Shane found the rhythm of his life through that whistle, and as he grew, his playing became more refined and clear. One day, randomly listening, the music sounded sweet, good even to me. We were older, Shane twenty-seven and I twenty-six, and on breezy nights where we found isolation away from the cabins and the others, we ate supper on the rails with plates in our hands, and after eating, Shane played. I looked forward to the sight of the small silver instrument, splotched with blackness from wearing with his fingers. Shane turned towards the water, his feet dangling over the waves, and played, letting the music ring over the churning waters, just as rich and sad as the rhythms of our lives, echoing into the abyss. And the night before we made it to New Orleans, there was hope in the tune, for tomorrow we were to step on land.

We sailed through a deep tributary of the Mississippi as the fading light sunk under the sunken land. The borders of the river were pale-green, flat, lined with cypress trees, and the air carried a natural swampy stench. A ghostly unease floated on the air, the feel that danger was near. Dangerous animals. Dangerous people. Here the sky appeared more compact than it did in Shannon or New York. Here the pink and orange colors of dusk came closer to the earth, and there was more land and water than sky. We were far into the muck.

The mosquitos began to bite only when the shoreline was illuminated by the glowing moon, and all around the ship, the crew were slapping their arms and swearing.

"Right nasty cocksucker," said Shane. "These little twats, festering like my body is slathered in chocolate." He slapped his neck. "Fuck off! Die with the blood of the Irish spoutin' from your butts, you fuckers."

Shane and I out-mastered all the other sailors in the art of dropping a fucken' swear word, and we knew the crew would laugh. The American sailors identified us as either the 'Irish boys' or 'those dirty fucken micks', and because of this Shane and I found clever ways to make ourselves known, the art of swearing being one which earned us good respect. We had no beer or wine since St. Augustine to helped us forget the mosquitos were there, and as far as pests go, the mosquitos had done more damage than any Confederate. After cleaning the deck, we went back down inside the cabins to avoid the bloodsuckers.

The cabins grew loud into the night. Benjamin of New Hampshire, likely worse than a Confederate himself, shared with us the only tale he'd ever heard about New Orleans. Said a friend of his had found himself hexed by a voodoo witch who'd disguised herself as a blonde beauty. This tale gave most of the natives in the crew a scare, though Shane and I didn't believe it only because Benjamin had told it. All the tales I had gathered from New Orleans spoke not of witches but of real women, who were not only beautiful but free of spirit, perhaps even a bit unholy as the Catholics say. I was raised Catholic myself, but hardly considered myself St. Joseph. I was ready for some solid ground beneath my boots, may the stories of witches be true, or the land be holy as heaven itself.

Two

The barracks in New Orleans were just off the river. We arrived midmorning and unloaded our necessities. The Americans complained about the odor, blaming the Confederates, and it was a foul smell. Steamy armpits and spoiled food with just a hint of death, rats or maybe even human. I wondered why none of the Union soldiers had cleaned up. The smell didn't take long to get used to, and after a while, its stench didn't reek so directly but came in subtle whiffs if you began to wonder why it didn't smell anymore.

We were ordered to have lunch in the mess with the Army troops. The Navy sailors stayed in their tribes, and Shane and I paired off as we were. Any of us that had arrived on the USS Empire had trouble stomaching the food because of the smell, and we were all anxious to go down to town. It'd been three weeks since St. Augustine, three weeks since the last beer or the last heart enriching conversation with someone who hadn't been trying to kill men in their spare time, or ready to kill at least. In times of peace, I took for granted these people or the sweet pitch of a woman's voice, or the flowing grace in the movement of her hands if she touched your arm with affection. Soft fingertips, not calloused like the formal handshakes a serviceman is required to make. The thought of her lips on skin made me light-headed. A life without this affection bred an anxiousness that can drive a man crazy.

When we were finally released, Shane and I went out and walked along the river towards the city. It was awful sticky outside, steamy and humid without a breeze. As we walked along the rocky shoreline, we came across a negro man fishing, free as a gull on a beach. This right well surprised us. As we kept on, we came across another negro man, walking as freely as Shane and myself. Then another. One negro, who was particularly well dressed in a seersucker suit, better than our outfits without question, even waved to us and said hello with not an inkling of fear in his eye. If you had told me earlier that we were in the same deep south as the horror stories we'd heard the black folks were living, I would have called you a drunk. It was clear this nastiness resided more in Mississippi or Alabama, and that New Orleans seemed to be a haven of sorts.

We came behind a market that stretched onward the length of several blocks, and lining it were buildings that stood three or four stories high. We were delighted to see so many people wandering the streets, filling the stores and cafes, living lives as though peace were known. In the center square was a beautiful Cathedral, the likes of which we had only seen in New York, and it was curious to me that God was living so far south, and that a church like this had survived the Union siege.

"Right," said Shane, looking up at the steeples of the church. "Time for a confession?"

"Right now?" I asked, "We haven't been here long enough to have sinned yet."

"You sinned plenty in St. Augustine," Shane said.

"It would be a waste of time to confess right now when we'll only have to go back tomorrow."

"You make a fair point. Still, back there we committed a fair bit of sin. A good Christian would wise up, wipe the slate clean tonight. Then He'll be more likely to forgive after the debauchery we're sure to commit here."

"I don't want to confess while keeping down whiskey from the night before."

"Wise beyond your years, my friend," said Shane, throwing an arm around me. "To think that I am older than you."

"Ah, yes. The experience a man can gain in only seven months."

"You say seven months as though it's no time at all."

"Seems less and less."

"Do you not recall that only three months ago, seven months separated us from the great Navy of the United States and that seven months before that, you weren't horrified to eat a potato."

"I was always terrified of potatoes."

"You loved potatoes. You only started being terrified when one knocked your tooth out."

"You remember?"

He placed a palm over his heart. "I couldn't forget that. The fondest of memories we've made together."

It was a somewhat humorous memory. We were young, the age you yank on loose teeth because you have nothing better to do. It was a foggy morning and we went down to the main road in Shannon and hid behind a tree with a couple of potatoes we'd snuck out from the ground on the way over. We waited, hiding and giggling until we heard the sound of a rattling cart and the stomping of hooves. The plan had worked before. The game was to try and hit the horse with a potato, and if you hit it just hard enough it would ninny and buck and break off into sprint while the poor bastard driving the cart swore like mad, grabbing at the reins, and speeding off down the road. This day was particularly foggy and grey, and we thought this would be advantageous, and smiles on our faces lit up when we finally heard the cart rattling down the road. It sounded old and rough, squeaking, and it was no wonder the old man steering was ancient and his mare, even older. God himself couldn't have delivered anyone more unsuspecting. The old sop's droopy eyes and arched back hinted he was about to fall asleep right there on the cart, the reins loosely gripped between his fingers. Once he passed the tree, I threw my potato and it sailed clear over the cart, arching into the long grasses on the other side of the road. A clear miss. Then Shane threw his, and the potato sailed up and fell down right next to the old man on the seat. He stopped the cart, and we went still though we should have run. The old man turned his gaze towards us trying to catch sight of our faces through the fog. He pulled himself up and lumbered off the cart as I yanked and urged Shane that we should leave, but Shane stood there with a big ole fucken' grin on his face, whispering and insisting that the old fart couldn't see us. Shortly after he said it, the old man cocked back and threw the potato as hard as his old arm could bear. It was invisible in the fog until the very last moment where it appeared right before my nose and smacked me in the lip. Coulda swore it was a rock the way it cast me backward.

"Serves you right, little shit!" The old man shouted. My head was cushioned in the dirt and eventually, I heard the cart clunking away down the road. I spit out my tooth in my palm and once the old man was out of sight, Shane laughed his happy ass off.

We opted out of confession and walked two blocks down the street where we came to a pub. It was glum, dark, and warm inside and there were only three men, the barkeep, a fat man sitting hunched over the bar, and a negro boy behind, cleaning glasses. All were sweaty, though the fat man was the only one sweating without working. We sat at two empty seats in the middle, ordered two beers, and the barkeep poured them from a tap.

"Where you fellahs from?"

"We're foreigners," said Shane.

"Mississippi?"

"No, but close. Ireland," I said.

"Ireland? Hell, I wouldn't even know where to find that on a map," he said. "What brought you boys down to Louisiana?"

"The Navy," said Shane, sipping the warm beer before him.

"Which one?"

"Who cares," Shane replied.

"Well, what made you join up?"

"The United States Government," I said.

"Damn pity. So you're Yankees."

We sipped the beers which were yeasty and unpleasant.

"Listen, boys," he said. "I ain't here to judge you if you ain't here to judge me. We all came off a boat from somewhere."

"Seems fair enough," said Shane.

"Enjoy the beer. It's on me."

"Thank you," we both said.

"A health to you," said Shane. "To more generous, sweaty gentlemen like yourself."

The barkeep forced a chuckle while Shane and I clinked our glasses and put down half the pint.

"Lawrence!" The barkeep shouted at the negro boy. "Keep your damn fingers out of the glasses. Business slow enough as it is."

"Sorry, mister Bruce," he said. His voice was deeper than expected; he sounded older than he appeared.

"Just go on back and clean the alleyway," Bruce said to Lawrence. "Go on now!"

"Yes, sauh..." said Lawrence with a nod before he left. Bruce didn't speak again until the back door to the alley closed behind him.

"I tell you boys," Bruce said. "I tried to do the right thing by bringin' im on. Figured a nigger boy could use a job just like everyone else. Then he goes and does shit like that." He went silent after saying this, as though contemplating his own thought, or waiting for us to do so for him.

"Shit like what?" Asked Shane.

"...Not worth the investment in my opinion....S' all I'm saying."

"Right..." Shane continued, "but what shit? What kind of shit made the boy not worth the investment?"

"You looking for business advice or you just asking? You saw him, didn't you? He kept puttin' his fingers in the glasses."

Felt like too much trouble to speak my mind considering the barkeep had gone out of his way to give us a free drink, and during times of financial hardship no less.

"Wasn't he cleanin' um?" Shane asked.

"Pardon?"

"Wasn't he cleaning the glasses?"

"I don't know what he was doin' with 'em. What do I care? What I know is that he ain't supposed to have his dirty fingers in 'em."

"You ever cleaned a glass before?" Shane continued.

"Is that a serious question, friend? I own a pub."

"So surely, you'd know that to get inside that glass, you have to use your fingers."

"I've cleaned plenty, and I tell you, I was able to do it without putting my fingers in it."

"Right. And how did you do that? Perhaps you could enlighten the boy."

"Since when do I answer to you? Are you aware, young man, that that's my name on the door out there....You understand me?"

"I'm just confused as to what he did that was so wrong," Shane said with a coy smile, sipping his beer. "I watched him."

"Bein' that I'm his employer, I'll decide what he does that's right and wrong."

"His employer or his owner?"

"Excuse me?"

"Why play dumb...You're good at playing the fool, but it's nothing to be prideful of, you know."

"I've given that boy a place to work."

"Oh, dog shit."

"Shane," I said.

"...You're out of line, boy," the barkeep said. "Now get the hell out of my bar."

Shane laughed as he stood. "You stupid git. Why bother saying anything? Why say anything at all if he was just working for a living like any other boy? You think you're hiding?"

The man reached under the bar and brought up a double barrel that he pointed right at Shane's nose. "There. You spoke your piece. Now I'm gonna' give you five seconds to walk out of that door or I blow your Yankee Irish ass to bits."

I felt that Shane was going to get in his final word. He always did. It was a compulsion.

"Shut your mouth, Shane," I urged, pulling him back. "Let's go."

"Thanks for the beer," Shane said, though spoke so much more with his glance, one which reminded me of my own father. A look in the realm of disbelief or disappointment. I'm sure my father was drunk every time he gave me a look like that and I always knew that he meant what his eyes were saying. That I had no power against him. I'd like to think that Shane's look drowned that barkeep in his own guilt, though I doubted such. I pushed Shane out the door, with the gun still pointed. We were inside long enough that back in the sunlight, we squinted.

I turned Shane around to face me. He refused to look into my eyes. "Look at me," I said. "Look! It doesn't make sense when the man's pointing a gun at your head. You completely mad?"

"What a worthless git."

"You're not even drunk yet!"

The city had an unpleasant smell of fumes from ships on the river and a steady whiff of mule shit. There was an occasional scent of roasted coffee. The source of the mule shit revealed itself when Benjamin turned the corner with his cronies Alexander, Michael, and Matthew. Matthew was the only one Shane and I cared to see. He never spoke much. Michael, however, was the only that truly scared us. Burly and beastly he was. He stood taller than all others on the ship, wider as well, with a thick black beard that covered his neck entirely, and his attitude, though not exactly predatory, was intimidating as though he framed his entire being around being able to scare others with a glance. Because of this, when most of the men on the ship were around him, they spent their words trying to earn his respect, sure that if conflict were to break out, he'd be on their side. Shane and I weren't so lucky as to have this type of insurance. He was prideful, a native New Yorker who loved his country as much as he hated foreigners or anyone who looked or sounded remotely alien. Even he, however, knew that Benjamin came from a more powerful northern family, and therefore, served him with pride. He was Benjamin's giant lackey.

"Lookit here," Benjamin said with his campy Irish accent he talked in around Shane and me. "A bunch of Irish foreigners. Drunk and sorry sights to look at. Don't you think?"

"Nice to see you, Benji," said Shane. "You're lips look chapped. Are you drinking enough water?"

"My dad raised dogs back in the country. They used to pick out the dumb pups and shoot 'em. My dad said the dumb ones could spoil the whole pack." His cronies laughed on command like well-trained dogs. "Shouldn't the Irish bastards be shot down like rabid dogs in the streets?"

"Good one," Shane laughed.

"Shane, me boy," Benjamin continued, throwing a heavy arm around him. "Where do these dirty southerners keep their women."

"Right in there," Shane said, pointing at the pub we just came from. "There's a sweaty one sitting all the way back. Very drunk that one. Just your type."

"Really, now?"

"I saw him myself," I replied.

"A looker….just inside. Christ, will you turn your face? Your breath smells like whiskey and cheese."

He brought his lips closer to Shane's ear. "Any niggers in there?"

"The whole city is crawlin' with 'em," said Michael.

"You'd never believe the Union took it," said Benjamin.

"You say that like you never see any in New York," said Matthew.

"Because," Benjamin shouted, "in New York, they at least have the decency to keep them all in one area."

"Oh," I said, "you mean like the Irish."

"Just like that. Yes."

"Alright," said Shane, lifting Benjamin's arm from around

his shoulder. "Enough affection for you."

"Come on now, Irishmen," said Benjamin. "Come have us for a drink."

"Afraid we can't today," I said.

"But why?"

"We have to go to confession," Shane replied, turning his back with steps towards the church.

"You're alright you two," he shouted at us, then turned back to his cronies. "They're alright, aren't they. Me two favorite fucken' micks in the world."

"Benji, I wish I could say you were my favorite asshole, but I've got my own to tend to," said Shane.

Benjamin hawed, then said, "I can't wait to have you boys shoveling ship of my shit."

"Ship off your shit?" Shane asked. "Is that right?"

"You know what I mean, you fucker."

"I can't wait, but bye-bye now, until then," Shane replied. He then leaned towards me and muttered, "Stupid drunken bastard."

"Hey!" Benjamin called to us. "You know that if you remain stationed on the Empire, I'll be your Lieutenant one day?"

"How may we show our care?" I asked.

"Follow—" he said and hiccupped. He belched. "Follow orders when they're given."

"I suppose if that day ever comes," said Shane. We started off again.

"Hey!" he called again. "There isn't enough room for natives and foreigners alike, but that doesn't mean that room can't be made if certain foreigners were willing to prove themselves. You micks are different."

Shane continued walking while calling back to him. "We're fighting in your war! What more is there to prove?"

"Where your loyalty lies!" Benjamin called back.

We continued down the city blocks, searching for a pub more social than the first when we came upon an interesting sight. There was a man, too old to be in the war, yet too young to be dead, and he sat on the case of a banjo he was playing, his hat flipped over on the ground before him. We stopped and gave him a listen. Shane was taken by the music, for he just had that rare, gifted type of ear that blamed itself in music's joys. He lost himself, his eyes floating upward to stare at the sky, dazed and unfocused, basking in the notes. After the man finished his third song, Shane dug in his pocket and tossed a nickel in the hat.

The moon had found its way into the late afternoon sky, floating between the narrow city blocks. We walked on, and before us was a large group of men, standing outside with drinks and cigarettes, laughing and talking. I walked towards them, sure that it was a pub when Shane touched my shoulder and said, "Look in there."

He was looking through the window of the small shopping boutique. Inside were two beautiful women smiling, oh beautiful smiles, conversing over a piece of cloth. One was blonde, the other brunette, both with their hair pinned back with the fashion, their dresses dark. Before I could even comment, Shane had pulled open the door and gone inside. I followed as any noble idiot would. He approached them, slowly but directly.

"Good evening, ladies," he said with a charming smile. Their beautiful smiles and stunning eyes turned to him, pleased with what they saw and heard.

"Hi," said the blonde.

"What's that accent?" asked the brown-haired one.

"Oh, you don't like it then?" Shane asked.

"I didn't say that," she replied.

"So you do."

"And what concern is it to you?"

"It's funny you should ask, considering you don't know who I am."

"Who are you then?"

"Shane Connell," he said, the smile back in full force, "and I wouldn't call it concern, miss. I've only known you long enough to be interested."

"Interested?" she asked with a chuckle and turned her smile to her blonde friend. "Where are you from?"

"The war…and you?"

"Baton Rouge."

"Charming town I hear."

"From who?" asked the blonde.

"My mate, Brady here," said Shane. "He's been there countless times."

"You think Baton Rouge is charming?" The brunette asked.

"…Deeply." I said.

"Why?" Asked the blonde.

"I've never had the guts to ask him until this moment," Shane said.

"What was your name again?" Asked the blonde.

"Shane, miss. And you?"

"Sarah-Beth," the blonde said.

"And where are you from?"

"Right here in New Orleans," she said with gleeful pride.

"It is fair to say that this town is charming," I said. "Despite being taken by the Union."

"I don't want to talk about the war," the brunette said.

"The lady has spoken…and what is the lady's name?" Perhaps it was my imagination, but before she spoke, her eyes appeared to turn on me, piercing but subtle.

"Gwendolyn," she said.

"Pretty," I said, "like the shade of green in your eyes."

"Brady!" said Shane, halting the conversation. "Shall we sneak into this pub next door and get the ladies some drinks? Ladies, what'll it be?"

"I don't know if we should," said Sarah-Beth.

"I want a drink," said Gwendolyn. "I want whiskey."

"But where will we go?" Sarah-Beth asked.

"We can go down to the river," Gwendolyn said, turning her eyes to Shane. "He can escort us there."

"For Miss Sarah-Beth…what'll you drink?"

"Gin," she said with a guilty smile.

"With limes," said Gwendolyn.

"We'll be right back. Brady."

"We'll wait, just outside."

We walked out when Shane threw a brotherly arm around me and we started inside the pub. "Brady, my brother. Dear, brother. Don't do that again."
"Do what?"

"Don't get all…I don't know. Romantic. Sweet. Especially with yours. Any tougher and that one would have a beard and a glass eye."

"I'm just trying to be friendly."

"Yes, and there lies the problem. Behavior, you see, not words. Actions, not phrases. Be sweet with your pelvis and not your mouth. Mouths are for being funny…among other things."

"Was it that bad?"

"Of course not. It was only what you said and how you said it."

"If you're sure," I said. Sad to say, I trusted him.

There were several people inside the pub, and the drinks took a decent time to pour. We hoped that the ladies would stay. We finally did retrieve the drinks and went back outside where they were patiently waiting with their charming smiles, both aimed at Shane which was obvious and made me anxious. Shane simply had a way of radiating a pure spirit, delightful energy which was both charming and humorous, and women lapped it up like kittens with a bowl of milk. I hoped that I appeared attractive simply by association. He suggested that we walk down to the river. I was silent as we walked, though at one point I looked over to see that Gwendolyn's eyes had drifted towards me when my gaze caught her by surprise and she looked away quickly. This happened one more time before the group reached the river, and I even grew comfortable making eye contact with her. We found places to sit along the shoreline, and nervously I sat next to her. Shane entertained, and we laughed for he did it well. Then, he told the tooth story.

"…We were crouched down, hiding behind a skinny tree, but it was foggy, and the ugly old man is bloody far away from where he launched it. Throws the potato at us, and fucken hard too. So it cruises through the fog, and then hits Brady here right in the fat maw." The women laughed. I rubbed my temples.

"So Brady flies backward, and the old man screams out 'You little shit,' or something like that, and then Brady looks up to me, and I think he's about to say something angry as though all of this was somehow my fault, but instead, he just looks up with his big stupid eyes, bends over, and spits out his tooth in his hand."

Sarah-Beth brought both of her hands up to her mouth. "Oh my God," said Gwendolyn, laughing.

Shane was chuckling now. "And he looks down at his tooth in his palms, and then up at me, like saying, 'Look what that old bastard did!'" Admittedly, this childlike impersonation of me was accurate. Worth the laugh. He'd physically stretched out his arms with a wide-eyed look of shock on his face. He looked like an idiot, as I'm sure I had.

As the night grew later, the sun's absence cooled the steamy air. The atmosphere between us grew more intimate. We moved closer together on the rocks, and the conversations grew deeper and quieter. Before long, Sarah-Beth's head moved onto Shane's shoulder and his arm wrapped around her. Her forehead moved towards his chin and he kissed it gently. Their eyes met, their noses came closer together, and once their lips touched, they showed no signs of parting.

I turned to Gwendolyn whose puzzled eyes nearly talked as if to say, 'do you think that we're going to do that?' My own questionable gaze returned something like, 'could be nice.' A lit gas lamp just behind us illuminated a bright shimmer on the water and reflected in her green eyes. They were a mystery to me. A cool and sultry channel to her secrets. I leaned in to kiss, and while she appeared confused for only a moment, her eyes then flickered upward into mine, and she leaned in, bringing her lips to mine. When she let go, I looked into her daring eyes again.

She looked down at my lips, bit her own, and we started once more.

The night had grown late. Drunk and joyous, Shane clapped and brought us to attention.

"Do you two live around here?" he asked.

"Yes," Sarah-Beth said.

"We'll come on then. We'll walk you home."

"Oh, that's okay," said Gwendolyn.

"Nonsense," I replied. We started to stand. Shane emptied his stolen glass, downing the rest of his whiskey, and chucked it, shattering the glass against a rock. I stood but stumbled backward a little and Gwendolyn put her hand on my back to catch me before I fell. I regained my footing and laughed it off, and she laughed too, but it sounded false. Shane belched and Sarah-Beth laughed, drunkenly.

We walked away from the river to the street which was lit by more iron gas lamps. The streets were far quieter than they had been earlier in the day.

"I'm uptown," Sarah-Beth said.

"Which way is up?" asked Shane.

"I'm over in the Marigny," said Gwendolyn. "It's just that way."

"Oh, good," I said. "I'm going that way too."

"So I suppose uptown is the opposite way?" Shane asked.

"How did you know?" Sarah-Beth said.

"My mind is a map. Brady, my boy. I'll see you back at the barracks."

"Well be safe, won't you?"

"Aw, my friend..." he said, throwing an arm around Sarah. "He's such a kind sop."

"He loves you," Sarah said.

"Damn right he does." He then told Gwendolyn goodnight and gave her a silly wave, and they began to walk in the opposite direction, Shane never taking his arm away from her.

Gwendolyn and I started to walk. I kept my hands tucked in my pockets, though I had the urge to take her hand. There

was a certain coyness and lack of surety in her expression, from
the heart or from the brain. I didn't love her, but I thought that
perhaps I could. The streets were barren and ghostly, parts lit
in splotches where the gas lamps flickered. Fear lived between
us, but fear of what? Of what might be in our minds and hearts?
I wondered what she could fear with the comfort of a capable
man beside her, a soldier no less, as I walked with her through
the blackness of night. Was the fear of me? That she could fall for
a foreigner? My mind was filled with uncertainty.

Her house was near, only a few blocks. She folded her
arms as we ascended the stoop towards her bright red front
door. Our eyes met as she turned around to say goodbye, and she
gave me a smile. But she struggled to keep eye contact with me,
and the smile quickly disappeared.

"Did you have a nice time tonight?" I asked.

"I did," she said.

"Good. Me too."

"Thank you for walking me home."

"Of course."

"Have a good night then," she said, giving another faint
smile before turning towards the door.

"Could I see you again?" I asked.

"There was a brief silence, and I knew her answer right
there. God knows what it was that I had said or did to warrant
such a rejection. I knew she was attracted to me in some way or
another, but it was over. She didn't need to say anything more,
but she did. She turned around and faced me.

"My father is a politician," she said.

"That's nice…"

"It's just that…I can only assume that you don't fight for
the south."

"I try not to fight at all."

"…Okay," she said.

"Not the answer you were expecting?"

"Not from a soldier…no."

"Well, I couldn't mean it any more than I do."

"That's no way to live," she said.

"It's a war. It isn't living. It's the opposite."

"Don't you fight wars so that others may live? Isn't that the reason there's war at all?"

"It's not my war."

"You're fighting in it."

"I do what I'm told and that's all."

"That sounds like cowardice to me."

"I'm not a coward. It's simply more important to survive."

"Well, I find that weak."

"Most American's find foreigners weak...even if we're not."

"So that's your excuse?"

"Not mine. Yours. Your country's."

"What do you mean?"

"Your father may be a politician, but let's not pretend that these talks of war are the reason he wouldn't approve of me. Sure, he's not alright with his daughter seeing a Yankee, but a Yankee and a mick? He wouldn't approve of me because I was born in a different place."

"You don't even know my father, or me for that matter."

"I know you're American and you natives are prideful of your land, but let a foreigner enlighten you. Your pride is unearned and we don't find it honorable. We Irish loved our land, but we were forced to leave. We had tradition on our soil. And here, where everyone is so proud, thinks they're so much better, there's been no time to make any tradition. No time to appreciate or value what you actually have here. Then you treat others who have it like dirt and make them fight your wars."

"That's not true, and you've insulted me and my country."

"Perhaps your country deserves to be insulted. Your people talk tough and then have thin skin when it comes to insulting their precious pride. An insult which may help to toughen weak-minded people like you and your father right up."

She slapped me across my jaw. It stung right horribly and echoed.

"If you don't like it here, go back where you came from. Stupid Irish bastard."

She went in and closed the door behind her. I stood embarrassed and alone but satisfied with having stood my ground. I walked to the river and along the banks to the barracks, thoughtful, and gazing upon the glare of the moon shining atop the black water. Staring at the Mississippi brought me back to childhood memories of the River Shannon, and I thought about how that place had framed me. I was the type of man that women slap, and despite this, I felt good about myself. Alone, but well. I reasoned that a woman wouldn't slap just anybody, but a man who could speak difficult truths. Staring at the river long enough, however, brought me back to old memories of my father. How proud he was of his land, of his work, and most of all, his bottle. I thought that he likely would have taken pride in being slapped by a woman, and the thought dampened my mood. Or I was just drunk…just like he would have been. Did he ever feel grief? Remorse?

I arrived back at the barracks and got into my cot. The room was vast, smelly, and dark, and all around me, I heard the snores of lost men. To be surrounded by men who in all ways but one were alone. I stayed up some time, thinking thoughts I didn't wish to think, waiting for Shane to return. More than an hour passed and he never did, so I turned over on my side and fell into a dry-mouthed, drunken sleep.

Three

Black clouds drenched the streets with rain, and I woke believing it was still night. Shane was still gone, and I was starting to worry. He was smart, but what were the dangers out there?

Shane's family, the Connells, were one of the three great shipbuilding carpenter families who lived off the River Shannon before the famine. Shane was one of the few of his brothers and cousins who preferred working on the ships the family built to building them. He reveled in life on the waves, and this began on my father's boat when Shane and I were young. The men in his family carried their long, wood-hauling history in their bodies, all of them moderately tall with broad shoulders and chests, with a certain intimidating stoutness about them that hid their soft-natured temperaments. Shane's father was the kindest man I had ever met in my life, and my family, the Gallagher's, had befriended theirs two generations before Shane and I were born. But our families' friendship only moderately compares to the one Shane and I had. A true brother, Shane was, and the only grown man I would die for.

I was relieved when he returned to the barracks around lunchtime. His clothes were dripping from the rain, and he wore a smile that hinted at mischief.

"There you are. Hell, I was worried. Where were you?" I asked.

"Falling for her."

"Sarah-Beth?"

"Oh, yes."

"The walk home went well then. It took you long enough."

"She is an absolute wonder, Brady...I feel so light inside," he said with a stupid, almost creepy gaze on his face.

"Are you still drunk?" I asked.

"What?"

"Are you drunk?"

"No, I'm not drunk. Brady, my boy, I've met an angel."

"Yes," I laughed. "What a divine creature...piss drunk on gin."

"It wasn't the gin, Brady. She loves me too."

"You've just met her."

"Yes, and it was no accident. I've known beautiful women, Brady. You know how the beautiful ones love me, but all of them may as well have been Quasi Moto, crocodiles, beast of the night in comparison.

"I want to be pleased for you mate."

"Are you bitter?"

"No."

"Now why are you so bitter?"

"I'm not bitter."

"Did it not go well with what's her name?"

"Not that it merits talking about, but no. Not particularly."

"Sarah-Beth said she wasn't so taken by you."

"Could have been nice to know before getting a right nasty smack to the head."

"She smack you then?"

"You know how the beautiful ones love me."

"There's beauty of a woman out there for Brady Gallagher."

"Right right. She's out there, all right, winding up her arm.."

"Don't be a cynic. You'll find her. And you'll find her when you least expect it."

"I'm happy you had a nice time. I'm hungry. Let's go eat."

"She made me breakfast."

"Again. That's wonderful. But *I'm* hungry.."

"She's a great cook, Brady. She cooks well enough to marry".

I chuckled. "Now there's something I never thought I hear from the mouth of Shane Connell."

Shane laughed too. "Truly. I was shocked when I had the thought myself. Even more so when I asked her."

I paused. Surely, as well as I knew Shane's humor, I had trouble laughing. "What did you say?"

"I asked her to marry me, Brady. We're to be married."

"Shane…are you serious?"

"More than I ever have been. I can't let her go, Brady. You have to take a chance on a woman like her."

"You already asked her?"

"Of course I did."

"Have you lost your head? Did you kill every brain cell in your head last night?"

"I felt certain about her. I've never felt that before. I felt it. I feel it still."

"What about the war?"

"—I'll feel it forever. What about the war?"

"Well, come on Shane. It's a war."

"It's not our war. We didn't come here to fight in a war. We came here for a new life," he said, struggling to take off his wet shirt which was sticking to his skin.

"I understand what you're saying Shane, but we're fighting in that war."

"And one day we won't be."

"So we can pray, Shane. We can't know though. We don't know how long it's going to last. Where we'll even be a week or two from now. Did you think about any of that?"

"I don't want to think about the war anymore, Brady. I don't want to think about the war, or the next day, or the next boring hour, staring over the water just waiting to be my own man again. I want to think about my life. I mean, what? Just because we're in this war against our wills, we're a slave to it? What's the reason to even keep going forward if each day that passes is spent serving my life for some old general or president whose face I'll never know. No, mate. They can't take this from me. Not this love. Oh, how I felt it. Probably the purest feeling I've ever felt, like listening to a song that steals you away from your thoughts, and leaves you floating in the middle of your life, stilled in awe. She's an angel, Brady. And while war can make men sad, or angry, or depressed, an angel-like her never can."

"It's a lovely thought, Shane. But its a fantasy, because come the end of the week, we'll be back on a ship and far from this land, and her."

"Aw hell, just be happy for your old friend." He dropped the shirt and it slapped against the floor. "Surely, both of us could use a little happiness after the life that's been chosen for us."

"I'm happy for you. I am. But how? How are you going to marry a girl who you met on the street?"

"Why does it matter where we met? We could have met somewhere else, and we'll meet again. The point is that we were meant to meet. I'll find her again after the war is over. And we'll pick a place to live and live there together." He said this and smiled as though the solution were not only obvious but simple. He faded away into his thoughts. "Can you see 'em mate. Little Shanes running around, making trouble...the little bastards."

There was such a brightness behind his eyes, a truth so deeply painful to witness. His dreams there were focused, maybe in desire, maybe something deeper. He was trapped in the fantasies of family life, surely his idea to reclaim free will when it was so suddenly snatched away, and to do so in the name of love. But it ached me to believe that these dreams were mere fantasy, for how else did our move to America start? Loading onto a ship with Shane, his mother and mine, and my sister, we too had dreams. Dreams of starting new business sure to blossom with the freshness of new land. Never once did we think that merely being young men would plant us in a war for another's soil, yet here we were. And here Shane was, divulging a new fantasy. What other option did he have? I battled to hide my hesitance for his reckless decision. It'd been weeks since I'd seen him so happy.

"Will she be true to you? Truly? Even if you have to leave and fight for a long time?"

"Come on, Brady. You're being so serious."

"Answer me, Shane. Does she mean it when she says she loves you?"

"I couldn't be more certain."

"As long as you are. It's still a war, Shane. If you bring that woman into your life, then you go out there, and God forbid you die, then what? Do you want that to be the last thing you ever do? Break someone's heart because some stranger wanted you dead?"

"This is not why I wanted to tell you, Brady."

"I know it's not. And I'm happy for you, I truly am. But once you do this, it isn't just about you anymore."

"You're being overdramatic. We've been at it for weeks and we've hardly seen combat."

"Please. I want you to answer."

"When did this happen? Don't you believe in anything anymore? Not even love."

"Of course I believe in love. Every day, I ache thinking about where my sister and my mum are, and what they think, and who they see. I want nothing more than to get back to them. And perhaps I could run, but something inside tells me that's not right. And I only say all of this out of love. Look at me, Shane. Tell me for certain that this is what you want to do."

I saw by his gaze that the words were potent enough, even through his urge to deny them and the questions they asked.

"I love her, Brady. I want to be with her. And if I can't promise her now, when can I? For as little as I want to admit it. You're right. We could go out there next week and never see this land again. I have to promise her now. It's all I have."

I felt pity, and how I hated that I did. Sure enough, he had that heart-wrenching look of a bright-eyed man stripped of joy, and for me to do it provoked a sense of distaste. I felt as though I'd sparked the desperation further, made him more aware of it.

"She spoke from her heart, Brady. She didn't hide what she felt. There was no senseless pride involved."

"I believe you."

"I hope you do."

"Well do it then."

His eyes lightened with a rejuvenation of the happiness he'd brought into the room, one which wouldn't again find full blossom, thought its restoration was indeed more true and more thoughtfully focused. He smiled brightly, then jumped onto me in an embrace.

"You're a dear man. The dearest I know," he said. "I'll love you until the day I'm gone."

"Don't say that. Find your girl."

He smiled wide again, eyes squinting. Then he turned, picked up his wet shirt, and walked away. After he was gone, pain leaked into my heart. I had a sudden urge to hit something, something hard that would hurt me back. Instead, I plopped down on my cot and was suddenly quite conscious of where I was. A large white room, grey cots in perfect order, only one crooked. I was aware of myself in the white room, alone. There, the truth of what Shane had said invaded my mind. His truths that we could be slaves to this war, that our wills were not our own. That such ideas could steal away love if we let them. These thoughts bred anger and it festered as I laid there alone in the white room.

Four

The next morning before sunrise, he'd snuck back, and I heard him gathering some things from his lockbox. I was awake after a weary night, fading in and out of dreadful sleep. I assumed he was off to spend time with his fiancé and that he'd be spending as much as possible before we docked off Monday morning, back to the blockade in the Gulf. Those days were particularly lonely, and I was restless.

I walked down to the French Market where I met a fisherman selling trout and asked him if he knew where I could buy a rod, or if he would sell me one. He was a kind old man and he asked if I was looking to buy for sport or commerce. I told him for sport he wagered a deal. He said that if I could catch anything of value, and I were to give it to him to sell, he would let me borrow the rod for free. I agreed and he went to his mule cart and retrieved a bamboo rod with an aluminum spool. Then he sold me some dead shrimp for bait. Before I left for the river, he asked me where I was from, and I lied to him.

My father was a fisherman on the River Shannon and twice a week he would sell fresh catches at the market. He made a life for us that way. All other days, he would take to the water with a crew of two other men on a boat, built by the Connells no less, and occasionally he would bring me with him. It was my dream and widely understood that I was to take over my father's small crew or have one of my own after he passed. He eventually did, but his business died with him. Still, those memories of days on the water were some of my fondest, and the fondest of my father without question.

I've often wondered if my spirit shared the same desire or necessity for life on the water as his. The endless and infinite rock of the waves had a calming effect on him. It made him peaceful in an otherwise angered way of living.

There on the bank of the river, I found a large, flat rock on a manageable incline. I climbed over to it, took a seat, and took in the river's power. It was angry. One of the more temperamental rivers I'd seen in my life, for behind it from where I stood, I felt its power rush in from the north. It carried with it, however, an illusion of gentleness, sounds of water shifting and breaking over itself as it rushed lightly onto the banks. The chaotic nature of the earth in a gentle, swaying motion. I hooked a dead shrimp and cast the line from the rock. There I sat and let my thoughts run free into the glare of the sun on the surface. My mind slowed. I thought of Shane and his love for that woman, and of how love makes men illogical. I thought of the pain my mother might be feeling without me there, left with the uncertainty of her imagination, and the horrible wonder if I was even alive. I thought of my sister and I hoped she remembered me, that she would remember me even if it would be years before I saw her again. I wondered if I had truly become a cynic and if (as Shane put it) this chosen life had gotten the better of my hopes. I wondered deeply, trying to remember if I had seen beauty in the world since the war had begun or if I had just found life's bitterness instead. I wondered if I knew what I wanted. A family? Children? A home? Or life as a womanizer? I tried to imagine myself as my father, and if I even could live my life properly, or if I'd simply be a reflection of him, with the bottle as my guide. Was such a life worth living?

It grew warm as the morning slipped into noon so I pulled off my shirt and let the sunlight beam on my skin. That warmth, along with the sound of the water, brought me to a somewhat peaceful state. A couple of hours passed before I hooked one. There was the exciting rush when the line jerks and squirms, where you settle yourself with focus. I honed in and reeled when the fish stopped fighting and grew tired. The fish broke the surface, sending a cascade across the top of the water, exposing his fat mouth, his scales shimmering in the sunlight. A fat and beautiful trout he was. I leaned over the river and grabbed him by the gills, took the hook out of his mouth, and held him up before me. My keep for the day. My father used to say that any day a man could catch a fish was a day he otherwise could have wasted. I understand how that could sound dramatic, but the feeling of it is pure enough to be true.

I decided that one fish was enough and that I had found what I was looking for. I cut a piece of the line and hooked the trout to it and flipped him over my back. Then I walked back to the French Market. The old fisherman made some fuss when he saw the trout. Perhaps it was just flattery, but he was very kind and went on and on about how he'd never seen a trout so big and beautiful from the Mississippi. I smiled, thinking how right he was that it was a beautiful fish, and his smile made me happy. I thanked him again for wagering the rod, and he offered for me to keep it, but I explained I'd be docking off in a few days and that I didn't have much use for it.

"Keep the fish, at least," he insisted.

"I couldn't," I said. "Take him home with you. Give your family a nice meal."

"Nice as that sounds, there ain't much of a family for me."

"Are they far off? Displaced by the war?"

"No. 'Fraid pneumonia took 'em long before the war. Wife and my daughter."

"Hurts to hear it."

"God has his reasons, I suppose."

"Get on okay then, will you?"

"I'll do what I can. Sure you won't take the fish, Mr. Brady?"

"That's okay…I'm sorry. I didn't catch your name."

"Martin," he said and smiled. He reached out a friendly hand. "You stay safe Mr. Brady."

He was a kind and friendly old man. Meeting him was

heartwarming. Certainly, it was a beautiful thing to meet such a man who'd lost all in his life, though still had his reasons to remain intact and not be bitter. I wondered how one could lose so much and still thank God for the chance. As for me, I was troubled as of late and questioned whether God even existed. To me, He was an idea, thought up by a couple of well-written geezers to make people believe that contentment and happiness were attainable somehow. When I pictured God, I saw the face of an old, wise man who, at best, resembled the good parts of my father; the qualities I wished to know him by. Was I ashamed that I never recognized him as a good man? How does a man reason with such logic and somehow find a way to thank God for the chance?

The answer was simple and clear to me. There was no God. You had your mother and father, and if they were good people, you were one of the lucky ones.

I went back to the barracks and had a shower under cold water. I found myself lost in fantasies as the chilly water ran down my back and I grew used to it, fantasies about what life would be after the war if I were to survive. These thoughts brought me comfort.

When I went back to the bunk room, Shane was there, collecting more clothes, and humming to himself. Something slow and full of sorrow.

He smiled a forced smile, finished packing, and left. He went to her and though I was alone, I was happy. I felt as though someone was still nearby.

Five

It rained hard the night before we docked out. Fat drops fell in loud and heavy splats, thunder boomed and lightning illuminated all for a second before the land went dark again. The cooks in the barracks, knowing well that many of us were about to depart, prepared a massive pot of gumbo, with fresh shrimp and vegetables, and they served it with stiff bread that must be ripped with your teeth. The gumbo steamed in the bowl with a small pile of white rice in its center. I put down three bowls. Shane was not at dinner.

We were each allowed two glasses of beer and I drank both of mine alone in my bunk. My head became heavy with either the beer or the looming reality of tomorrow, going back to sea. A return to the water and return to the war. I took life from the water, but despite my usual affinity, I liked New Orleans, and the thought of a stable life there danced sweetly in my head. A simple life it would be. I was sure that Shane was imagining such a life himself.

He returned about an hour or so past midnight after the rain had stopped. He must have thought I was asleep because he climbed up into his bunk without saying anything. I sensed something was off, and sure enough, after several minutes, I heard stifled crying. I thought it better to say nothing, though I wanted to comfort him. But sometimes crying is the only solution.

I slept a few hours but was awake when the sunlight started to bleed through the windows. Many men were already sitting up in their bunks, thinking heavily, and it appeared that it had been a night of light and useless sleep for most. When I rose, I looked over to Shane's bunk where he was tucked away, fast asleep with eyes tightly shut, mouth agape, drool leaking onto his pillow. I smiled.

Those who remained asleep were awoken when the officers called us to attention. Shane finally awoke, and you could see a brightness about him that was absent just the night before, either hope or something else to get him through the morning. He looked over to me and nodded with a dip of the chin, and eyes ever dreary but bright.

"Ah, mornin'," he grumbled.

"Morning mate."

"Alas the day has come when we pitch away our debauchery and take back to the sullen seas, full equipped with wasted time, and fantasies of good food and women."

"I'm trying not to think about it."

"And naturally, all we'll have is time to think."

"Best get started. We don't appear to be the only ones moving slow today."

Then it was time to make our way to the docks where our ship, the USS Empire, loomed above us. She looked well, certainly better than she had the last time we stepped aboard. She stretched over seventy meters down the riverfront, the dark-cherry redwood faded in spots, and the raised sails a faint yellow. The two-hundred or so men lined up before the bridge, pacing slowly over the water to their fate. Some carried muskets, leaning the barrels on their shoulders, and some wore covers on their heads. All had similar lethargic expressions in their eyes and on their lips, the corners of their mouth cast downward. There was a grayness in the clouds and on our minds. The line aboard her moved slowly.

Once aboard, we went down to let off our things, then came back to the deck to await Captain Harrison's orders. He was a just and wise captain. He led with a stern voice, only soft enough to never detach him from his humanity, and he had an important understanding of war, it's chaotic and oftentimes tragic ways. We waited only twenty or so minutes before he emerged from his quarters and stood before us.

"At ease," he said. "Good morning."

We all returned a rather pitiful "Good morning."

"Again! With energy!"

"Good morning!"

"Seems I've done myself a disservice standing downwind of your mouths. I smell more beer and whiskey than air." We chuckled with little energy. "Fortunately it seems you'll have some days to recover. We will travel back southwards to the Gulf where we'll join a few vessels in guarding the mouth of the river. A fleet of our Navy will take up the Mississippi in just a few days and head northward towards Memphis. The President as well as the General believes that our best chance of shutting off transport and communication between Confederate ports is to take them, one by one. Our job is simple. We defend the mouth from Confederate interference. Sit tight. We'll eat some lunch, and we should port off some time shortly after noon... Gallagher. A word, please."

My stomach dropped a bit. I'd only had one conversation with Captain Harrison before, and was surprised he remembered my name. The men began to disperse back down towards the cabins to the food line by the galley. I went the opposite way, up the stairs to the upper deck.

"Reporting, captain," I said.

"At ease. How was your week Gallagher?"

"Great, sir."

"Good."

Suddenly, it came to my attention that perhaps he'd received bad news about my family. Such thoughts had evaded my mind until I looked into his eyes.

"Is everything alright, captain?"

"I'm afraid not. Lieutenant Thomas has been sent home. He contracted a nasty fever and the doctors don't believe that he'll live to the end of the month. He wants to spend the remaining time he has with his wife and son if he can make it back to Philadelphia in time."

"I'm sorry to hear it."

"I have nothing against foreigners, but understand that if I were to promote you directly to Lieutenant, my higher officers would not be pleased. Maxwell will become a Lieutenant, but someone must take his role as a Junior. I need a competent man who knows how to sail and can earn the respect to lead his contemporaries, and you were the first name that came to mind. I'm going with my gut. You'll be responsible for giving orders during combat to your crew and to command this ship on course when needed."

"Me? You want me?"

"You, given that you're open to the responsibility. Are you?"

I paused. "Of course, Captain."

"Don't think me ignorant Gallagher. Know that I expect this will be a challenge considering you'll be dealing with a bunch of angry natives, but know that it's not my responsibility to give a rat's ass what the natives think about my decisions that I know are best for this ship. Lead them. They'll come around when they believe that you have their best interest at heart, which I believe you do. Is this all ringing clear for you?"

"It is, Captain."

"Good. Of course, you'll be granted full citizenship and at a later time, we will discuss your salary. Understood?"

"Yes, Captain."

"Good. Report to duty."

"Thank you, sir."

"Serve your country proud, son."

Pinpricks sprouted up my arm. The sheer unexpectedness of the news made my headlight and my stomach full of anticipation. I went down to the galley, but I was hardly hungry, perhaps out of excitement, perhaps out of fear. I watched the ignorance on their faces as they began to brighten with life at the quick acceptance of a changed but familiar reality. Our time in New Orleans was over and we, the men, would find a way to live and continue on through darker days. I stood behind them as they jarred and joked with one another, and I was terrified, for their lives were now, at least partially, under my command.

I took a bowl of stew and a piece of stale bread and went up to find Shane sitting in our usual spot on the deck. He had a brightness in his eye that I hadn't seen in days, and he even smiled upon seeing me.

"Well then?" he asked. "Everything okay with the Captain?"

"Yes," I replied, poking at my stew with the spoon. I clenched to hide the smile brewing behind my lips.

Shane took a bite of his bread and it crunched. "You alright there?" he asked, mouth full. "You thinking of something dirty?"

"Dirty? No."

"Then why then? Why the shit-eating grin?"

"You're not going to believe it."

"Try me."

"Captain Harrison promoted me."

"He what?"

"He promoted me to Junior Lieutenant."

"You're shitting me."

"I'm not."

He punched my arm. "That's great, Brady!"

"It's alright," I said, no longer trying to hide my smile.

"Alright...I'll smack you once you finally pull your head out of your ass. This is great news. You've got to be one of the first Irish Lieutenants in the American Navy. Maybe even the first."

"It's a lot to take in."

"I'm sure, but no doubt you're the right man for the job."

"That's the part I'm not sure about."

"Well, you are, otherwise he wouldn't have promoted you."

"How will I earn the respect of the natives?"

"I don't know. With time? Buy them a beer the next time

we port. You'll figure it out."

Lost in thought, I stared out at the water. I was happy, but I was nervous. I was certainly thankful that Shane was there to tell, and that, even in the smallest possible dose, there could be a celebration.

"You're worried, aren't you?" Shane asked.

"At least a bit. Not two days ago were we talking about how this war wasn't even ours. Now I'm supposed to help lead the effort."

"Half that job is already done. They have to take orders from somebody. Besides, this proves what we already know."

"What's that?"

"That the Irish can do many things better than Americans. Not simply just out drink them."

"Benjamin is going to be furious."

"Yeah…I can't wait to see his face."

"He may try to start a revolt."

"No doubt, they'll be a couple of hard asses at first, but they'll settle down once they see that you were promoted for a reason."

"And what reason is that?"

"You're a hell of a sailor, Brady. You know it, as well as I do, that you were born for a life on the water. Maybe the best quality that your father ever gave you."

"Think about it though, Shane. People could die if I make a mistake. Because of me"

"Oh for the love of Christ, quit worrying and take a bit of pride in yourself. True, some of these men could die, Benjamin or Michael included mind you (which who would mind that) but you also could very well succeed in this, and even more possibly save lives because of it. It's an enormous responsibility, I'm not denying that, but hell Brady, you could be a real hero when all of this is said and done."

"That's a nice way to think about it."

"It's how you have to think about it. Honestly, think about what Captain Harrison must see in you. He's responsible for lives too, you know, and he's wise, wise as he is old. Some wise old fucker would not have picked you if he didn't think you were capable, but he knows. You know the ship. You know the sea. You've been around it your whole life. You're more ready for this than you think."

"Yeah," I said, believing such words he spoke. "Yeah, that's right. Only I don't know war."

"What man does?"

"Plenty who have to lead men into one."

"The concept is fairly simple. When you think about it, there are men on one side, men with different opinions on the other, and both sides kill each other until both sides eventually share the same opinion. You just bring these men together. You can. You've done it with fishing crews, you can do it with these men. They're eager. They want to fight. Make them want to fight under you."

"I'm glad you're here," I said. "You have a way of making me feel good about myself."

"Since when?"

"Today may be the first day, actually, but it's the best day you could have picked."

"I'm proud of you, mate, not to get all sentimental. But I am."

"I'm proud of you too."

"Oh, none of that."

"Shane, honestly. We could have crumbled. Neither of us expected that when we stepped on land here that this is what would be in store for us, but here we are. And not to get sentimental, but one of the only reasons I can bear it is that you're right here with me because, to be frank with you, when I pictured America back in Ireland, I thought of fresh land and a new life. I was stupid. I thought we'd make our own way because we wanted to. But while you're here, I don't mind fighting this war, because I fight it for our families up north, waiting for us to return, and I fight it for you."

"Not to get sentimental though."

"Right. But I'll have your back out here. We'll keep each other afloat, and then you can have your wife, and we can have our land, and we can make something as we dreamed about. A simple life with some wives, maybe a couple of lads, and a hairy dog to chase."

"You let your dreams get the best of you, mate."

"Tell me it doesn't sound grand."

"It does. And I believe you when you say we'll get there. Let's just take it a day at a time, yeah?"

"Alright. A day at a time. But we'll get there, Shane. We're going there."

"I know we are. Anyways, congratulations, mate. I have no doubt you'll do a fine job," he said, leaning in, giving me a quick, strong hug, then pulling away to hide his affection.

Amplified did the waves sound, splashing against the cherrywood of the ship, recoiling and sprinkling the water back down upon itself.

"Is the captain going to tell the crew, or are you?" Shane asked.

"Well…we'll find out."

"I suppose so."

He turned out toward the river and lifted himself up to sit on top of the rails. Silence channeled between us for a moment before he pulled the tin whistle out of his pocket and began to play a slow tune.

The first note always took me by surprise, how the beauty of it was always so high-pitched and ghostly, yet the sound still sweet. I listened as the sound moved downward onto the surface of the water and synced with the crashing of the waves. Such harmony between the sounds of the whistle and the light break of the waves brought with it a harrowing atmosphere, a pain of what was, wispy darkness in the near future, but a certainty that forward was the only way. Never did I so long to move forward into the inevitable, hopeful even of what was to come, sure that something bigger than us both lied ahead, though let it be said that this feeling did not come without fear. I was lost in the tune when Captain Harrison appeared. He waited until Shane came to a stopping point. "That's a nice song there, sailor," he said. "Quite nice, indeed."

"Thank you, Captain."

"I take it you've heard the news."

Shane looked to me. "I have, Captain."

"Good," Captain said, before turning to me. "Well, Lieutenant. Let's get this ship moving southward."

"Yes, Captain."

He gave me a nod and walked away. My nerves wrapped tightly around my innards, though Shane stood right there beside me, and there was strength to take from him, offered freely.

"Shane," I said.

"Yes, Lieutenant," he replied, slipping the whistle back into his pocket. He looked up at me, smiled.

"You're on lookout. From the nest."

"Yes, Lieutenant." He brought a salute up to his temple and dropped it along with the smile. Off he went to the nest.

I walked slowly outwards to the top deck, above the lower where most of the men were sitting with near-empty bowls of stew. They laughed and talked loudly over each other. The thought of looking into their eyes made my nerves jolt the stomach, hesitant to speak as I now had to. My hands trembled. My throat felt blocked with phlegm.

"Attention!" I said. The laughter and chatter died down quicker than I imagined it would. Their silence was deafening. "I need all hands on deck."

The silence was their reply. Their heads were swaying between each other and shrugging shoulders.

"I said all hands on deck!"

"We heard you the first time," Michael said with indifference.

"Since when do you say anything?" Benjamin asked.

"As of now. I've been promoted to your Junior Lieutenant."

Benjamin laughed a half humored, half-serious laugh.

"Are you joking?"

"Lieutenant Gallagher!" Captain called from the upper deck. "Set the course!"

The word "Lieutenant" I heard muttered before me, under the breath of all the sailors, trying to confirm what was surely the day's joke. 'Is it true?' I heard one man ask. Their questions brought on the vulnerability of being naked in the cold.

"Your father is going to love this," Michael said to Benjamin, loudly. Comparatively, I felt like more of an outsider than when I first stepped onto American soil.

"All hands on deck!" I said.

"But we haven't brought our bowls back down to the galley," a man named Dekalb said.

"Well, bring them down then."

Only then did some of the men begin to move, some with more urgency than others. Others sauntered by and treated the orders as temporary demands. Others as a silly mistake. Benjamin remained seated, his eyes flickering between the soldiers in motion around him, puzzled that any order that had come from my mouth was being followed.

"Let's move!" I ordered. "We're to set the course south down the river."

Some men still refused to follow and for them, I was lost and ignorant in my response. My impulse was to weigh the anchor under sail and take on the mistakes as they came. The time allowed for no other method. My heart raced, my mind imagined the Empire cracking its bow on the rocks of the shore. All I could do was give proper orders, the same which I had never given before.

Men began coming back up to the deck from the galley. I remained on the upper deck and stood a distance from the captain who was behind the wheel. I began giving my orders.

"Lay aloft and loosen said!"

"Lay aloft," a man called back. "Loosening sail!" Said another.

"The braces are not untied!" Someone shouted.

"Cease!" I shouted back. "Sorry! Untie the braces, now."

"Give them time," Captain leaned over and whispered.

"Yes, Captain."

My head turned towards the masts where I watched the men work, now with effort. Once it appeared the braces were untied, I started again.

"Loosen sail!" I called.

"Loosening sail!"

On the deck below, the men lined up on the posts of the capstan. "Starboard forward braces!" I called. There and then, those braces fell. "Port main mizzen braces!" I called, and there such braces fell. I looked towards the captain and he gave me a nod. "Weigh anchor!" The cluster of men shifted as they forced themselves onto the posts of the capstan, and slowly the wheel began to turn.

"Heave!" Michael called. "I say this only so you don't have to hear it from the filthy mouth of the Irishman." He cried his heave between every few steps of the rotation. The chain of the anchor cranked and the ship began to lean towards the starboard side.

"Hoist up the topsails!" I called.

There they fell. Captain Harrison himself worked and turned the wheel of the rudder. There had been many times in my life where I had been aboard a ship as it began to move, though never was I met with the light-headed sensation which came from the grandness of watching the land move away, like God himself had gripped the surface of the earth and began to turn it over in his palms.

"Hoist the outer jib!"

My focus now turned to the water. The river was low, so I planned to direct the ship to its center where we'd stay the course until we reached the mouth. There was a gratifying feeling, a certain pride in watching the men respond and work together, though I knew that simply giving basic orders on how to move the ship would not be enough to earn their respect. That alone was far off-course.

The top-wind was heavy so we swiftly coasted down. The sky was grey and overcast, and the swampy lands leading out towards the gulf were muddy and drenched from the rains of the prior night. Gnats swirled in black clouds, filing into open mouths. The further south we moved, the cooler the air became. Colder days were coming.

We reached the sea in just over four hours. Now there would be downtime on the water, waiting, listening to the barking, and complaining of sailors like cranky grandfathers remembering times of the past. However, the men were strong. The waters had strengthened them. And they were self-righteous, fighting for the country they loved, or the land they held sentiment for. They fought for what they believed to be nobility. The thought that their singular existence would make a direct impact on the world, or nature itself, for war itself is in a man's nature. Nature is not so compassionate to avoid such tragedy. Our world was now the war. Never did I dream, hope, or imagine that I would be leading men into such a world, but here I was. A world that was natural none the less, and the same nature that allowed potato famines. Human nature. Nature lacks the compassion that God himself is supposed to provide. Only a fool could be fooled by the idea of God in these waters, a fool lost to sights of beauty.

I looked up and saw Shane in the crow's nest, casting a thoughtful gaze out onto the waves. Perhaps nature did have some compassion, for friendship was also an act of nature. Baking in the sun, perched in the clouds, alone with thoughts of lost love. He looked forward to war with looming pain. Such is genuine nobility. I felt his aching down on the deck like a dreadful cold. He attempted to conceal these splinters, needing a hope to rise into the atmosphere like steam. Sarah-Beth was on his mind no less—the wonder if she would wait for his return, or the few memories he'd made from their nights together. He basked in those memories, for they were a heavenly fantasy in comparison to the life we moved forward towards. His pain rained down from above like cold, hard rocks of hail, and in no way could I bear the load. It was his alone. There are certain times in life where the sea can heal pain, but this was not one of those times. Isolation is no remedy for lonely and desperate men, for the feeling of loneliness is only amplified by the sea. A man's life requires stillness and solid ground beneath his boots if he is to heal from loneliness, not a steady rock in isolation. Such infinite motion and the sound of the crashing waves only intensifies that ache of emptiness, that motion which has outlasted every life on earth except the life of the earth itself. Its sound is one that's unique, rich, and alive, like good music, because it too carries lives with it. It is the sound of absolute motion, and for a man to heal from loneliness, his life requires stillness. I worried about Shane. I truly did.

Days passed, and the waves continued on.

Six

The days were long, and we grew bored. The countless hours spent in silence among the group after our jokes became contrived or went stale, and the thoughts inside our head were loud, and men began to think about women. Women we imagine. Women we once knew.

I believe I have been in love once. The girl's name was Alice and we were fourteen when we met. Her father was a simple man who cleaned fish at the docks for a few pence when times were good and used the meat to feed them both when times were not. Her mother had died, but she never told me how. When the housework was slim, Alice went to the piers with her father. An evening after a day's work with my own father, I caught sight of her as we came back to the land, and after that night, I never failed to notice her when she was there. She was beautiful to me, her head full of long auburn curls, a face full of freckles on the smooth skin of her cheeks. She was the only girl I'd ever seen who was unafraid to touch a fish fresh from the water.

I'd finally built up the courage to talk to her. I introduced myself as a fisherman, boasting while doing so, and she didn't appear disgusted so eventually, I asked her if she'd like to take a walk down to the river. She said yes with a smile that I'll never forget. She walked over to her father and told him she was going to take a break, and his gaze turned to me. He gave a subtle wave and a head nod, and many thoughts were communicated through his eyes, one of which was the imminent threat that fathers give young men. I went up and shook his hand and introduced myself, and he asked if my father was the fisherman by the same name. I said he was.

"Has his boy working already, does he?"

"Yes, sir. Since I was about twelve."

"Well, then. Good day on the water?"

"Yes, sir."

"Let him know if he ever needs 'em cleaned, I'd be happy to provide the service."

"I will, sir."

"As for you…bring her back in an hour."

"You have my word."

"Good. Off you go then."

I gave him another nod, turned my look to her and she smiled again, into my eyes with her own. They were eyes of dark green and glowed in the fading sunlight. We started off, walking slowly along the river, the trees and green grasses passing on our left, the boats coming in on our right. We were quiet, for I was nervous, and the light, tickling fear troubled me. Spending time with a girl was something that at that point I'd only daydreamed of. Her hair shimmered in streaks of white light as she turned away from the sun.

"I've noticed you," I said.

"You've what?"

"I've noticed you. Out on the docks with your father."

"Really?"

I nodded. "Is that strange?"

"No," she said with a smile, and she reached over slowly and touched my hand. I felt it trembling lightly. "I've noticed you too," she said.

"What did you think?"

"Many things. I mostly just wondered who you were." At this, her cheeks turned red. "How I could talk to you."

"You wanted to talk to me?"

She turned her eyes away from me and nodded.

"You could have talked to me," I said. "I'm not much of a talker though, but I would have talked to you."

"I'm glad you did."

"Did what?"

"Talked to me," she said.

"I am too."

All went quiet again. We heard only a couple of distant gulls cawing to the sky, and our shoes moved and crunched the gravel beneath our feet. The silence grew uncomfortable again. The back of my throat itched and felt stunted, and I cleared it quietly. I flipped my hand to grip hers, though my courage was not enough to squeeze. I swallowed and the feeling in my throat remained. I took a deep breath, wrapped my fingertips around hers, and she caught them and held them tightly in her own. Her hands were cool to the touch and soft for a girl who spent her days scaling trout.

I walked us over to a distant tree and we sat down, never letting go of each other's hands. The clouds began to change colors and cascaded in yellows, oranges, and pinks. And our hour was nearly over, though it felt too soon. The time incomplete. A light breeze rushed in, blowing gently the strands of her hair. Her eyes looked back to mine and my own held her gaze, and in that instant, all fear was gone, floating away with the clouds of dirt that moved down the gravel road. I leaned to kiss her and she met me halfway, and her lips were gentle. My head was light, and my arms wrapped around her. She let go of my hand and placed it on my thigh, and I grew tight, and I felt as though she loved me.

Three years later, Alice and I were engaged to be married. I stopped working with my father as much, and many times found myself at her father's house doing handy work he had trouble doing because of his age. I helped clean fish at the docks. Her father, as simple as he was, seemed a happy man, or as happy as a man can be after losing a wife. He was a good man and I hoped for the day I would be a son to him, and a husband to his daughter. But such a day never came.

I thought about her often on the sea. Those memories brought me joy, though the foundation that supported them was based almost purely in sorrow. I needed strength, for my mind awoke in unease morning after morning, as I harshly remembered that any day I could lead these men into combat. The sunset reminded me of that bank in Shannon, kissing the first girl I ever loved, and even with the pain that such sight evoked, every sunset still led to relief, for we had made it another day without taking fire.

There was the possibility that the Confederates would strike at night. In the darkness, perhaps it was even more likely that their ships would try to run the blockade. Though nostalgic memories made me feel as though the sunset was a sight of safety, there's was no guarantee that it was.

The evenings were nice however when we'd break for supper. Over time, Shane gained some of the life back in his eyes, and again were we able to joke and talk...though hardly, if ever, about women. He made fun of some of the sailors on the ship, and I listened, unable to contribute. I refused to give them a reason to hate me even more than they likely already did.

He was leaning over the rail of the ship, playing a song on the whistle, when suddenly there was a burst of water, and a splashdown from below. Gave Shane a right scare and he scrambled backward away from the water. Then another. I inched over and looked out towards the gulf to see a group of dolphins, playing, jumping, spouting water from their blowholes. I laughed at Shane and called him back over.

"What is it?"

"Look at 'em!"

"Scared the right piss out of me, with their big stupid noses."

"I like them. They seem peaceful."

"Sure...if they don't give you a heart attack."

Thereafter, every evening, I scanned the waters looking for more.

Shane continued to play as I went off to use the head. My

attitude was bright as I thought of dolphins, thought of peace as I stepped further down into the bowels of the ship, and it was dark for sunset was upon us. The porter had not yet lit the lamps. I reached the door of the head when suddenly there was a great sense of unease that took me. I paused and looked around, and in the corner, in the darkness, I saw a slight movement.

"Who is that?" I asked.

He started to laugh, his tone deep, his voice grumbled. "What's the world we live in when the newest appointed leader is still so terrified of what sits in the shadows."

"Michael is it?"

"Scared of the dark like a young tike, yet he leads men into war for a country that isn't even his own," Michael stepped out into the faint light there was. He loomed over me like a titan, his ground claimed, his threat pure simply with his presence. "Seems someone thinks that you're more than just some stupid mick."

"What is it you want?"

"Hmm. An explanation. Granted, I never thought I'd be the one to be promoted, but even I thought I'd be picked before you. You see, people usually tie you to your family, and if your family repairs shoes, well, people will think that's all your worth. But my father, he's a small man. My tall blood comes from my mother, and believe you me, my father lives in fear of my mother. Tall blood. Now there's an interesting idea for the blood of a leader. A large force that stands before everyone else —like a wall. But captain doesn't seem to think that way. He thinks that the best leader for our company is some mid-sized mick from foreign lands. And for what I ask? Why are you the one?"

"I can sail."

"Hmm. Washington could sail too. But he could also kill, and when I look at you, the last thing I see is a killer." He approached, rapidly and gripped me by the throat, lifting me up against the wall. "So I ask, what do you see when you look at me?" He began to squeeze. "Do you see a killer?"

I used one hand and gripped his wrist, and relaxed as far as I could. He wouldn't cut off my air supply and it told me that this was a tactic intended to scare. Nothing more.

"You won't kill me."

He squeezed harder. "Oh, won't I?"

"No," I struggled.

"And why not?"

"Because you know I'm not your enemy."

"You seem so sure about that."

"Because it's true. You know I'm not. So why then is your hand around my neck?"

"Because I am a killer."

"Let me go."

"You don't think I'll kill you."

"No."

"Are you sure?" he enforced, squeezing harder than he had.

"Yes. You won't be tried for treason over me."

"Tried for treason for killing a mick?"

"Your lieutenant. Whether you like it or not. Now let me go. That's an order."

I stared at him and saw all the hate in his eyes, for how he hated that he couldn't kill me. He knew it. I kept my eyes there with his, and slowly he lowered me down, my feet touching the floorboards again. He shoved my neck slightly as he let it go.

"This is wrong," he said, pointing his finger at me. "You have no right to lead this ship."

He began to walk away. "Michael," I called. He turned back with his forced and hateful eyes.   "When the time comes, you should know that while I won't fight and kill for my-self, I'll do it for you."

He approached me rapidly again. "Will you dare to lie in my face?"

"I don't lie."

"My father died for this country, for his land, for his people. And I rue to think of what he would say if he saw this horse shit taking place on this ship right now."

I looked at him with all the humanity I could muster. "My father died in a bottle. He didn't die for anything honorable, and he's the last person I want to be."

"Ah, but see. That's your blood. That's who you are, slimy and destined for that same bottle your father died holding in his palms."

"You don't know that."

"Neither do you. Hell, what's to stop you? A couple of American boys that you hate? We won't. We'll watch you drown. Be sure of that."

"I won't watch the same. Perhaps that's why I'm your leader."

"I ought to kill you with my bare hands right now."

"Do it then. Kill your lieutenant."

He smiled, taking some twisted joy in the thought no less, or perhaps even humored my surety. Still there, as he stood on the banks of laughter, I kept my face straight, hiding my weakness. What could he do, other than kill me?

"If you think we'll take orders when the time comes," he said, and while I held there, expecting more, he said nothing else. His smile remained as he turned and gently shook his head, walking up the stairs back to the upper level of the ship, the wood crackling beneath his massive feet.

My heart was pounding in my chest. My hands trembling. I felt lucky to be near the head.

Seven

"How could you try to kill me?"

She stood there looking down at me, disappointed. A blank expression. I was her son and I had tried to kill her. And I was frightened because I had no answer, no reason to dispute that I wouldn't have finished the job. As far as I knew, I had tried to kill her, and why I failed, I didn't know. I was remorseful. Burdened with guilt. I had an urge to cry. I felt it build in the back of my throat. Then a bell rang, but mum, she didn't react to the sound of that bell. I heard it, though. It rang again. She stood there looking down at me, so disappointed as the bell grew louder. More rapid and louder still as though the sound itself was detached from the world around me. She began to weep.

"Why? Why would my baby boy try to kill me?"

How I stood there with no explanation. What was to be said? Physically I was constricted, unable to speak even though I wanted to. I urged desperately to scream into the grayness of night. "I didn't, mum. I wouldn't!" But I was unable to say so. A bell rang again.

"How could you?" She cried, "I gave you life!"

A wave from a black abyss appeared behind her. How pained I was to see my poor mother's face in such a hellish setting, after so many months of missing her. Why here, I thought? Why now? The wave of dark water wrapped around her as she screamed and it stole her away. I cried, dreadfully. Another bell sounded.

The sound of the bell woke me. I wiped my damped eyes rapidly. I was surrounded by the wooden walls of the cabin, as the bell continued. Men were rising from their cots with urgency, many leaping and stomping across the floorboards as they rushed to slide on pants. It clanged on with no rhythm, rung by a panicked hand. The guilt from my dream was still quite alive within me, though more real panic was slowly starting to take its place. I rushed to get dressed, then went up to the deck where men were swarming into position with little order. Voices were loud and scattered, and though many talked, hardly any communicated with each other. The air outside was chilly and damp and the fog was grey and thick. The men scrambled like ants in a pile that had been kicked.

"Gallagher!" I heard, called through the chaotic noise of the men.

On the upper deck, I saw the captain loading a musket. I went up to him, tripping and catching myself on the steps as I climbed.

"What's going on, Captain?"

"Confederate ironclad! About five hundred yards off," he said. "I want men on every port side gun, and those who aren't down there, I want on this deck with muskets loaded and ammunition at the ready. They're headed straight for us."

"Are they trying to run?"

"Why would they come straight for us if they were trying to run? Go!"

"Do we have backup, Captain?"

"Nine hundred yards east. We have to hold strong until then."

Down on the lower deck, the men were still scrambling into place. "Man the guns!" I called. "Man the guns! Man the guns! Jameson, Wallace, Douglas, Pendleton, David, Shane, Dekalb, Michael, and Benjamin, down to the lower guns with me! Everyone else, get your muskets up here and prepare for battle!"

A watch called from the crow's nest, "Four hundred yards west!"

"Now!" I called, "Let's move!"

"They're moving quickly!!" The watch screamed.

"Steam engine," said the captain, coming up behind me. "We have no time to piss around. Have your weapons loaded and prepare to fire!"

As I walked down the steps to the lower deck, I squinted and tried to see the enemy ship through the fog. We may as well have been blind for hardly could I see the waves of the black waters below crashing into the wood of the bow.

The men took their orders. My nine moved down to the guns beneath the deck. I heard the captain shouting behind us. "Christoph! Get us turned port side so we can get a shot!"

We came down into the dark cool gunner's deck below the ship and began preparing the gun. All my men were there, but Benjamin. Even Michael was. "Behind the port side guns, Michael. Portside. I want two men per gun, and do not fire until I give the word." He stared at me for a moment and as I had the night before, I held my eye contact. He sighed, gave a slight nod, and went to his gun.

Shane approached and asked, "Are you alright, mate?"

"We'll talk later. Man the back gun. I'm with you." Shane nodded and went.

"Where's Benjamin?" I called, only to be met with silence. "Where is Benjamin?!"

"I haven't seen him, Lieutenant," said Douglas.

I gave my hand a blow of hot breath and did all possible to settle my mind. The ship started to lean starboard side, and I went up to the window to see if I could see the enemy thought the fog. Still, there was nothing but fog and black water.

"Are we loaded?" I asked.

"Almost, Lieutenant."

"I guarantee they already are." Nervously, I gave my hands another blow. The bell above began to ring again, and I heard the muttered cry from the crow's nest, "Three hundred yards west!"

"Armed," Shouted Michael. "We gonna kill these rebel cocksuckers or what?"

"Hold steady," I said.

Stomping boots descended the stairs. I assumed at first that it was news from above, though I realized shortly after that it was Benjamin coming at a leisurely pace as though showing up to a game of cards. I approached him urgent and tenacious.

"Where the hell were you?"

"Who do you think you're talking to? I'm not going to die following the command of some fucken foreigner, who loves this country just as much as a dog shit stuck to the bottom of his shoe."

"You want to do this now?"

"That a threat? Michael, do you believe this, the way this scum dares talk to me? Piss off."

"Listen to me," I said. "Put it aside. We need these guns manned."

"I said piss off you fucken mick!"

Shane appeared from no-where, pouncing like a lion, and outright tackled him into a wall. "Enough of you, you right prick," he said, picking himself up, dusting himself off.

Benjamin jumped up just as quickly and charged him, "I'll kill you…"

I stepped in, wrapping my arms around him to hold him away from a fight. He squirmed and fought back, his anger pulling him in every direction. "I'll die before I take orders from you foreign shits!" The rest of the crew gathered around, swarming him, pulling him further from the fight.

"Is this a joke?"

"Piss on this shit!" Said, Michael. He went face to face with Benjamin, who was now held back by four men, grabbed him by the collar, and pulled him close. "Listen to me, you selfish dog! I'm not about to die for your fucken' pride, you got that? Man your fucking gun, take the orders, or jump overboard before I kill you myself."

"Let go of me!"

He pulled Benjamin's nose right to his mouth. "I shit you not, you bastard, if we survive this, I'm going to kill you in your sleep, go back to Baltimore, and fuck your mother if you don't take that man's orders. Understood?"

"So much for loyalty," Benjamin retorted. "He's a mick! A fuckin' Irishmen. He doesn't care about the war. Why would he? He's not an American."

"We're all behind a gun now. American, Irish, Nigger, or Chinese. Be a man, or don't." He let go of the collar and gave him a hard shove into the other men who caught him. Then all went oddly calm, quiet. Michael turned to me. "What's our orders?"

It was quiet but the waves splashed on. Then the ring of the bell and a cry of "Two hundred yards!"

"Prepare to fire," I said. The men aside from Benjamin stomped off to their cannons. Benjamin walked. I went to the window and looked out again, seeing first only the black waters below and thick fog above. The cold air brushed against my cheeks. I squinted, and saw it, for like a monster from the gray abyss did it appear. A rounded black ship with an iron shell about it, the red flag of the Confederacy waving, perched up from its bow.

"We have sight of the enemy!" I shouted. "Hold your fire!"

I held my wrist to stop the trembling in my hands. The barrels of their guns were aimed for our eyes, and four men on top of the confederate ship aimed rifles. Even with a clear shot, as they had, they did not shoot. Why did they hold fire? Were they waiting for us to strike first? Why would they not shoot?

"Orders, Lieutenant!"

"Hold!"

"Are you out of your mind?" Benjamin called. "Their aiming right for us."

"I said hold! They're not firing."

"It's an Ironclad warship," said Benjamin. "They're going to ram us!"

"They're not firing," I mumbled to myself.

"We're fucken' sitting ducks! If we die..."

"Hold I said!"

I moved close to the window once again, peeking through. Guns were still pointed but the man at the highest point of their upper deck had taken off his shirt and waved it wildly above his head, and he was skinny and had a terrible wound slashed across his chest. This ship had clearly felt the tolls of war, and possibly this was a wave of surrender. Perhaps they didn't have the gun power. Perhaps not the manpower. It seemed clear that surrender was their intention. Silently, perhaps even with cowardice did I pray. Once again, dear God, let us avoid this battle. Why I prayed, I could not tell, but pray I did, silently and alone.

A cannon boomed to my left and I jumped as did the beating of my heart. Then came a gruesome crashing sound. Scanning around our deck, my heart sunk deep, but our men appeared okay. My head was light, and I was unsure who had fired, them or us. Then I saw Benjamin, breathing heavily behind his smoking cannon, the smoke like wisps of death, moving inward. Benjamin turned a gaze to me, an expression of firmness, confident, even proud, in his defiance. I peered out the window to see the blistered damage the ironclad's shell had taken. All appeared light and dreamy. Then the battle began.

"Fire!" I cried.

The guns boomed in quick repetition, jutting back after ignition. Each shell struck the warship, though the crashes were muffled and distant. The Confederate soldiers on the top deck of the ironclad ducked down before returning to an upright position with their muskets aimed. They began to fire.

"Reload!"

Bullets zipped through the cracking wooden boards of the lower deck, rushing by us. The cracks and crashes violently sounded all around us. We ducked to avoid the bullets, all of us but Michael who paid them no mind, lumbering swiftly without fear, grabbing shells from the pile to reload the cannon.

"You idiot!" He yelled to Benjamin. "If I get through this day with my head attached, I'll chop off your balls and feed them to the sharks."

Another bullet pierced the lower decks near Benjamin's position, and he yelped in fear, falling backward. Cool air came in through the fresh bullet holes.

"Reload, Goddammit! Prepare to fire."

We could hear muskets firing from above.

"Benjamin, you bastard," Michael cried again.

"Fire!" I yelled.

The repetition of cannon fire sounded off again. After the boom was the sound of the shells penetrating the hard iron of their warship. Smoke filled the cabin with the smell of burning gunpowder. Then another boom sounded from a distance amongst the zipping musket shots. A shell suddenly crashed through the wood only a few meters from Shane and me and struck Jameson in the knee. His leg cracked backward, and his upper body went forward, and he cried out with a scream that made my chest light inside before his head slammed into the wooden floorboard. He went quiet.

"Reload!" I shouted.

"I need relief," said Dekalb, who had just lost his partner.

"Shane, get the gun loaded," I said.

I went to the pile to retrieve a shell for Dekalb. As my back turned to the enemy, another round of musket shots pierced through the cabin. Away from my sight, I heard Michael scream. I picked up the shell, turning to look at him as I returned to Dekalb's gun. Michael was gripping his shoulder as he stumbled away from the cannon, holding tightly the wound. The crevices between his fingertips were crimson with blood, and the wound itself appeared almost black. "You fuckers!" He cried out. I loaded the shell into Dekalb's gun, then hurried to make my way back to Shane.

"Medic!" I called upward.

"Can we fire?" Wallace asked.

"Bet your fuckin' ass!" Michael screamed, a grumble of pain in his throat.

"Fire!" I shouted.

The cannons boomed. Shells were heard crashing into the water, far less striking the ironclad.

"I won't die until all you southern shits are dead!" yelled

Michael.

"Reload."

"Cover!" Benjamin suddenly squealed. Then another cascade of musket shots fired, though far less than before.

"How do they have such a solid shot on us?" Pendleton asked.

Michael screamed a curdling howl of pain, bending over with his hand tightly gripped on his shoulder. The warfare stilled for a moment as they reloaded, so I went back to the window to look.

Their ship was right there, hardly ten meters away from our own, and moving towards us with daring speed. The muskets of our men from above were firing in a final attempt. "Get down!" I shouted, jumping down to the floor to cover my head with my hands. Some of the men had a chance to follow my lead, but most were simply confused. The clad struck us, and the men standing were cast across the ship. Wood cracked and splintered loudly, as though it were the cracking of a tree trunk itself. Above, one heard bodies slamming to the deck of the ship. I tried to regain my composure, pulling myself up to my feet, but the floor was leaning towards the hull. We were lucky to be afloat, and possibly would not be for long.

I coughed through smoke. "Sound off! Sound off!! Michael, are you okay?"

"I'm just barely okay, Lieutenant," Pendleton said.

"Keep it that way. Where's Michael?"

"Piss on this," said Benjamin.

The others started sounding off. "Shane?" I called.

"I'm alive, Brady."

"Who's hurt?" I asked.

"Aye!" said four of the men.

I stumbled over to the port side window, for the ship was clearly at a lean. The ironclad was out of sight. Then the daze slowly started to wear off, my full consciousness and attention awoke by sheer panic. They had bull-rushed us, so I quickly moved to the starboard side and peeked through the window where I saw the big black monster again turning wide as to reset their aims on the opposite side. There on its port side, a burette of cannons pointed right for our eyes. I felt they were about to fire as though it were a sense for the aim was only too right.

"Stay down!" I ordered.

"Why?" Benjamin asked.

Then they came. Three booms. Three shells soared towards us and crashed through the wood of the cabin. Douglas took a direct hit in his back as he was standing, and shattering bones sounded like thick oak branches breaking under pressure. He made an inhuman squeal, and the last sound he would ever make.

"Rifles!" I called. There was no time to load the guns on the opposite side.

"Lieutenant! Douglas is dead!"

"I know he's dead!" I shouted, filled with rage. "Shut your mouth and load your weapon."

A couple of shots fired from up above us. I went back to the window and saw that the ironclad was straightening its course. We were due to take more rifle fire if they had the men and ammunition left. We needed a retaliation at that moment.

"Fire!"

My men pointed rides from the windows and began to fire. After they did, I finished loading my own musket and aimed outward where I locked on to the very same man who'd waved his shirt in surrender at the start, his horrible wound still visible through the fog. I aimed for the wound itself and fired. The smoke fogged from my barrel, but I had missed him.

I turned my eyes around to check again on our progress. "When can we fire?" Someone asked. Then Michael collapsed forward after trying to stand again. I went to him and struggled to flip him onto his back. His shoulder wound was deep, black, and fresh with purple flesh and black blood. His eyes rolled upwards. The whites in his eyes. He was sweaty and smelled raw and sour. I touched his cheek and it was cold.

"Michael," I said. "Michael, stay with me. Medic!!"

Benjamin fired off a shot. A few more men fired after him. I turned and looked to Shane who was finishing a reload. Then he brought the barrel of his gun up and aimed out of the window. Before he could shoot, enemy fire came through. The bullet cracked and splintered the wood before him into a hundred pieces and he went down, dropping the weapon. My heart fell with him.

"No!" I shouted, quickly leaving Michael to rush to him. "No, Shane!" I went down to him and slid my palm behind his head, and he settled, and it swayed limply there in my hand. Lying there on the wood, he used both of his hands to hold his gut where he'd taken the fire. His bottom lip was slightly bloody and quivering. So were his hands, and when he lifted one of them from the wound on his gut, it was soaked with blood. I looked into his eyes and they looked back at me wide with shock and desperation. He moved his hand back to the wound and softly he touched it.

"No," I muttered to him and myself. "No, Shane. No."

"Lieutenant!" Wallace called.

"Just stay here with me," I said gently. "You're going to be okay. You're going to be okay, mate."

"Brady..." he said through forced breath.

"I'm going to get a medic down here right away, okay. You just hold on, alright mate. You hear me..."

"Brady!!" Wallace shouted again.

"You hear me, Shane?" I asked again. "Do you hear?"

Through purple quivering lips and wide eyes, there was only shock and pain.

"Brady!" Wallace screamed. "Something's wrong with Michael!"

Turning around to look, I saw Michael with convulsing, slipping into a seizure from loss of blood. My head grew light, and I was immediately nauseated. Gently, I laid Shane's head down on the floor. I stepped up and went to the window, only to see the man with the wound lifting the barrel of his smoking weapon down below him to reload it.

"Who has a loaded weapon!" I shouted. A tear ran down my hot cheek. Silence was the only response. I turned back to Michael who was still convulsing on the floor, and there I saw his rifle lying by his side. I leaned over and picked it up, cocking back the breach as I walked to the window. I brought the barrel out and set my sights on the scarred man who had just shot Shane. The cold air blew calmly on my face. I sucked in a breath, and for that moment, my trembling ceased and I went still and focused. Aiming again for the wound itself, I fired, and the bastard took the shot in his throat and fell.

I dropped the rifle to the floor and turned to see Shane still trembling there. A good sign. He was alive. "Arm the center starboard gun," I commanded to the others.

"Do we have time?" Pendleton asked.

"Do it!"

"Michael is dying, Brady."

I paused, overwhelmed entirely. Looked down to Michael who went still and dead. I held everything in for the moment, tears involuntarily moving down from my eyelids. "Load the gun now!"

Wallace and Pendleton held endless questions in their eyes. I quickly moved back to the window to watch and wait for the moment that the ship was in our path. Muskets continued to fire from above.

"We're armed, Lieutenant!"

"Hold," I said.

"Rifle fire came in through the cabin, and I remained still. If I were to die, this was as good a time as any. I refused to duck or flinch.

"When do we fire?"

"Not yet," I said.

The ironclad moved towards us, preparing to take another charge.

"When do we fire, Brady!"

"I said hold!"

Shane then gave a horrible cry from the pain. The sound

made my chest light, my face tight. My eyes swelled with tears. I bit my lip and focused on the ironclad. They continued to move forward, and when they came into the path of the center gun, I shouted loudly, as though trying to drown out his cries, "Fire!"

The cannon boomed and the shell sailed, striking the clad in the center of its upper deck.

"Pick up your rifles and fire at will!"

And then I rushed back to my friend. Down on a knee, I seated myself on the floorboards behind him, lifting his head and shoulders to cradle them in my arms. I slid his back to rest lightly on my chest. His cries had dissolved into a shaky whimper, but he was alive and conscious. Though the desperation in his eyes had evolved into fear, I held him. He would not be alone. I held him in the hope that together we would share some courage. He struggled to inhale, a high-pitched gurgled breath. An exhale seemed like relief before the struggle to inhale once again.

"Christ," he said in a forced breath. "It hurts, Brady. It hurts to breathe." He trembled.

"Relax," I said. "Just relax."

"Wallace, Pendleton, and Davis still fired from the windows when there were three booms in the distance, all in unison. More cannons. I adjusted myself to block Shane from the blow, expecting an impact.

"Backup!" Wallace shouted, a celebration in his voice. "A Union cruiser. They sent backup!"

"They finally came!"

Shane struggled more with each breath, but I spoke to him with all of the hope I could muster. "The backup is here, Shane. You hear me? They'll surrender, the bastards. The bastards will surrender." I tried to force a smile.

"Brady. When you get back." he inhaled a clogged breath. "—When you get back, you find her."

"Who, mate?"

"Sarah. Find her."

"I will. I'll take you to her. We'll go back to New Orleans

and get you fixed up and the two of you will be together."

"Find her," he struggled to breathe through phrases. "Tell her. What she meant. I love her, Brady."

"The battle's nearly over. We'll go back to the city tomorrow."

His cold and trembling hand gripped my own, but it was weak and wet with blood. He moved his hand to his shirt, shaking as he slipped in his pocket. With all the strength he had, he pulled out the whistle.

"What's this?" I said, touching the whistle which trembled in his palm.

"You're my brother. You're my friend."

"You are my brother. You're always going to be my brother."

He forced a pained breath, then went still as he exhaled. The whistle stilled in my hand as he let go, his hand falling lifelessly on his torso. The terrible breathing sound stopped.

"Shane?"

"They're doing it. They've surrendered, Brady!"

"They're waving white!"

"Shane?" I asked again, hardly expecting an answer but hoping. "Shane. Come on, mate." I shook. "Come on."

"Brady?" someone said. "Oh, no."

"No, Shane." I couldn't stop the squeal in my throat. "Shane, no." His body was still. I shook him gently so he couldn't feel the pain of the wound, but there was no pain to feel. Behind calm and dead eyes, there was no one. He was gone.

"We had to keep going mate," I said tears in my eyes. I forced a smile, lost in a dream. "Our boys were supposed to make trouble together, throwing rocks at horse carts. Those bad Gallagher and Connell boys who always make trouble."

The pain in my chest grew, with every thought urging him to live. Upon the ceasing of gunfire and warfare, once again, I heard the settling calmness of the crashing waves. They would continue on forever. Shane was gone and the waves continued on. I squeezed my friend's body as the ship rocked.

Part Two

Alone

Eight

According to the captain, the three Union cruisers arrived just in time to swing the objectively small battle in our favor, only right before we risked losing the ship entirely to damage from the ironclad. How the Empire remained afloat was a mystery, strange like death, for the Confederate clad had nearly ripped the hull right off. The rudders were gone. There was cannon damage on the masts. She'd suffered greatly and the only thing to credit her ability to float, in the mind of Captain Harrison, was the grace of God himself. The Rebel clad however had taken only two rounds of cannon fire from the arriving ships before their crew finally waved white. Just in time as it was said. Just in time. Their remaining men were captured and taken aboard the largest of the three cruisers, and they would be taken back to New Orleans to be imprisoned. The two other cruisers towed us to a small town called Grand Isle where we would plan our repairs and decide on arrangements for the dead. There would be a wake in two days and our men would be buried at sea.

We woke early the next morning, and the repair crew began repairing the hull of the Empire in preparation to sail her back to New Orleans. The rest of us were given the duty of preparing the dead men for burial. We transferred them to the alien Union cruiser, far larger and primmer than the Empire, named the USS Frontier. We lined them on the upper deck, laid side by side. Jameson, Michael, Shane, and five others whose names I did not know. We embalmed them in soft, white cloth and covered the pale hue of their cold skin. We wrapped their faces, covering closed eyelids. When we were finished, we brought them down into the Frontier's storage to keep them cool until the next day when the burial would take place.

Us living still had to sleep aboard the damaged Empire due to lack of space, not that it mattered. Since watching the life leave his eyes, I couldn't bring myself to sleep. Any rest was more of a fade into a semi-conscious state, riddled with haunted thoughts which only grew more detailed until their horrors woke me entirely. My mind was ridden with the picture of poor Shane below in the ship just meters away from ours, still and covered. I was haunted by the thought of tomorrow when we would leave him behind. How much I craved a drink and fantasized about how I would have one when I made it back to New Orleans.

I wondered how I would find his Sarah-Beth. The sorrowful, near-excruciating thoughts of my friend fired through me like shells from a musket, and only stopped when I could no longer hold back the sobs in silence. This feeling came in a piercing urge to howl tears which would only wake everyone and show my weakness.

The morning was near and true sleep was impossible, so I stood, dressed, and went up to the deck to the rails near the bow, the same place of isolation where we would eat our meals, and Shane would play the whistle. I stared out onto the ocean watching the black water, the unlivable holy ground. Over time, the sky's color began to change, first to grey, then to orange, until the blueness of day rose to take over. Maybe an hour passed, or slightly more before Captain Harrison came out of his quarters earlier than any other man and carried with him a wide plank of red-stained wood.

"Good morning, Brady," he said.

"Morning."

"Would you like some coffee," he said, leaning the red board against the rails.

"Alright then."

Captain then retrieved two tin cups of coffee from his quarters and brought them out. The sun had begun to rise, and we were quiet as we sipped. My head was heavy from lack of sleep but the coffee felt nice going down. Steaming hot and slightly bitter. We drank while leaning up against the rails.

"Cigarette?" Captain asked.

"Sure."

He handed me his which he'd rolled and lit it with a match before he started rolling another.

"The board?" I asked. "What's it for?"

"Hm. Yeah. A plank for the burial. Attaches to a latch between the rails. Leans forward when you pull a chord. I stained it myself the morning after Fort Sumter. We lost many good men that night prior, and I spent the night thinking about how I could honor them. I thought that since plenty of effort goes into making a casket, that a sailor at least deserves some effort, being if it is only a painted plank of wood. So, I keep it with me. Honors them in my opinion. Many great men have been buried off that there plank."

"Thoughtful then."

"Try to be as best I can," he paused to let the finality of life settle. "Were you able to say goodbye? To Shane I mean."

"I don't know. Tried to I suppose."

"You may not see the value in that now, but being able to say anything in those last moments is luck." He sipped his coffee again before lighting his cigarette. "I lost a brother when I wasn't much older than you. He was different than I was. Far less adventurous. Didn't seek to see the world as I did. No, he was content with a quiet life close to where we grew up. We're from Virginia, and when he grew up, he went west to work in the coal mines in Appalachia. We fell apart for some stupid reason or another, and off he went, met a woman, had a daughter and a son who I never met. But he was a good man and a good father. Then he died. A collapse in the mine and that was it. I never had the chance to say goodbye. I never even said it to the boy who was left to grow and have a family, never said it when he was alive, and he passed on as a man that I would never know. He had a whole life that could have been a part of my own before I went to sea. There probably ain't much more that I regret than that, not saying goodbye to my brother."

I listened without speaking.

"People live for a reason," he said. "And there's a reason we say goodbye. There's meaning in goodbye. I don't know what it is, and maybe it ain't my place to know, but there's a reason. Hopefully, that will leave you with something."

"He left me this," I said, pulling the tin whistle from my pocket.

"What is it?"

"His stupid whistle. He used to play it when we were young."

"Is this the same that he would play out here on the deck?"

"It is."

Captain Harrison took it in his hand and observed it. "Quite the gift. I read once, though I don't remember where, and granted, its a bit dreamy for my taste, but I read that music is that soul's way of speaking. Maybe there's truth to it, or maybe not. I'm not one for spiritual talk, but hell, I like music, and I've yet to meet a man who doesn't. Fills people in a way that nothing else quite can. You have memories with this, don't you?"

I nodded.

"Well, hold onto it then," he said, handing it back, never quite peeling his eyes away. Surely, he'd noticed the bloodstain. The captain lifted the tin cup back to his mouth and emptied it, took a puff, then flicked his cigarette into the water.

"I'll wake the men."

He went. I looked down at the whistle and toyed with the idea of playing, but the thought of doing so was painful

Men began to move about the ship, and once dressed were ordered to board the USS Frontier which would sail out deeper for the wake. Once aboard, we brought up wooden tables from storage. Then we had breakfast before we sailed out about an hour south into the Gulf. Time coasted as the ship moved, and its passing hardly felt real, but dreamlike and full of sorrow. Few spoke. All followed orders mechanically without much thought. Once the land was barely visible, we anchored. Then we brought the dead men up to the deck. We carried them up on canvas gurneys, and there were only two gurneys so we had to make many trips. Then we laid them on wooden tables on the upper deck. Captain Harrison went aside and put the stained cherrywood plank in place on the starboard side of the ship towards the ocean and not the land.

Eerie it was how we could tell who was who among the dead just from the shapes of their bodies through the cloth, and the small tufts of hair sprouting from the wrapped crowns of their scalps. Shane was the furthest bag to the port side. As the living surrounded them, they, the dead appeared sacred, and clear it became how we had gathered to honor, not their deaths, but their lives. Our glumness hung on the air. All went still just before the wake began, and the captain turned to face us after glancing at the sea to collect his thoughts.

"There was a pastor who spoke at my father's funeral…a boring ole snot, but he did speak a verse that's stayed with me over the years. He said, 'We fix our eyes not on what is seen, but on what is unseen, for what is seen is temporal, but what is unseen is eternal.' I think it's from Corinthians, and I believe the verse regards where our fear of death comes from, that is, our lack of knowing what's to come. And any time there is fear within you, expect that you'll have to find courage when you least feel able. I've lived long enough to know that, and it's a sad truth, but a truth to life non-the-less. Nothing can speak to the courage these men showed. They stared down fear with reddened and emboldened eyes and faced it outright. Gave their lives for it. Let us not forget that they lived such a life, and how valiant of an end it brought them. Through you, your stories, your memories, these men can be immortalized as well as honored and loved."

There were silence and stillness amongst the living,

more of us than had even known the dead sailors, for the crew of the Frontier were among us. Waves crashed about the ship. A grey cloud dimmed out the sunlight, giving the atmosphere a color that matched the faces of every living man aboard.

"I want to give anyone here who wishes to speak the opportunity. Take as much time as you need."

All remained still for only a moment more, when the most unlikely person stepped up before us. The porter named Jacob who I'd never heard speak a word before, stood before the tables, his hands crossed at his waist as he held his trembling wrists. His eyes shied away from our own out of nerves. He trembled, but it was clear, he was determined, driven by something higher than himself.

"I. Ummm. Mi. Michael was always. Ki. Ki. Kind to me. Not to. To. Say that anyone else ha. Ha. Has. Was mean, bu. Bu. But Michael was always ki. Ki. Ki…kind. He told me funny jokes and wo. Wo. Would give me. Gi. Give me extra bread. Even once I. I. I. Sn…snuck into the galley and got him mo. More. Be. Be. Because he was hu. Hungry. He was a goo. Goo. Good man, and all. All. All. Always hungry and I hope he's in a be. Better. Hea. Heaven."

I heard Benjamin mutter something as the boy stepped down, and the anger it filled me with gave me surety of murder. I wanted to hurt him more than I ever had before, but judgment won me over. It made me pity the living and made me believe that perhaps there was a reason that Shane, or no. It only made me angry.

Wallace then raised his hand and said, "I'd like to say something." Captain gestured him to the front of the floor.

"I watched Michael die, something horrible. I'm sorry. That's too much to say, I think. Captain talked about courage, and I can't think I could think of a better word to describe who Michael was. Fearless. He would say anything to anybody, whatever he was thinking, and it made people love him. I wish I could have known him longer, you know. The only time we were able to spend time together away from the war was in

St. Augustine and just then in New Orleans and both of those times were great. Some of the best in my life even. He was just one of those men you can't forget, not while he was living and certainly not after he's....well, dead." He bit his lip. "That's all." Wallace turned to the bodies and finished by saying, "Rest in peace, friends."

I knew that I should say something about Shane. What stopped me, I don't know. More men went up. Another spoke of Michael. One then of Jameson. After he stepped down, I caught sight of Captain Harrison out of the corner of my eye, looking back at me, a signal of fed courage and pureness.

So I went before them, Shane's clothed body behind me.

"Nothing can change this," I said, and all was unbearably still. "No-one should die this way, but still, that can't change what happened. One of these men was a great friend to me, you all know which one. That doesn't sound like enough to honor who he was. Because he was more than that. He was someone I loved. He was a reason to keep on living. And now he's gone... He's gone. Why can't I wrap my head around that?" The lump returned to my throat and I held back. My eyes dampened. My voice began to break. "He was a funny man. He loved his family and he was just like his father. Christ, I'm sorry. I'm so sorry, Shane." I caught my breath and wiped my eyes. Why was it so damn unavoidable?

"He was a good man. A good lad and he died in love with a beautiful woman. I'm going to find her and tell her what's happened. And I suppose life will keep going. I'll find a way for him."

I turned. Away from the men and walked to the side of Shane's table. I looked down at the lifeless body, his arms crossed within the cloth, and I touched his arm. "Thank you for the life you lived. Goodbye, my friend." I let go and wiped my eyes again, then walked away from him.

The sound that followed was near silence, only the sound of the water. Captain gave the order with a simple nod of the head and Thomas and Wallace lifted the first man, Jameson, and brought him over and laid him gently on the plank.

"Rest in peace, son," Captain said. He pulled the line, dipping the plank, sending Jameson's body into the sea with a calm splash.

When Shane's time had come, I went to help carry him. We placed him down and the weight of what once was in my palms now laid peacefully on the plank. "Rest in peace, son," said the Captain. Then he pulled the line.

<h1 style="text-align:center">Nine</h1>

The morning after the wake, the repair crew had managed to repair the Empire enough to have it towed back to New Orleans by the Frontier. Our crew was to be stationed there for a month, for Captain Harrison would not abandon his ship. Grief floated on me, and the mere sight of the barracks brought painful memories. After only two nights there, I asked Captain if I could take leave, just until we were called again to the blockade. He granted me a temporary sabbatical, and I moved to an inn on the outskirts of the city, and though the city was familiar, it was not the home that I so longed for, desperately.

I remained distant from everyone. The only love I felt at that time was when I thought of my mother or sister. I ached for them. I imagined often abandoning my post by jumping a train back north, an escape from this barren desert of the soul. Most nights I struggled to sleep, and this deprivation made me sickly, irritable, and eventually, I grow angry. If by chance I slipped into a nap for an hour or two, I considered myself lucky.

I found my haven in the pubs, for sure as Shane was dead were their people in pubs surrounded by others who had nothing. We shared this, though we remained distant strangers from each other. All of us searched for an escape, from something or another, and where we found this was our drink. I'd sit in a pub even if I was fading in and out of sleep, for as loud as the pubs were, my thoughts were never louder than when lying in blackness, alone in bed, trapped with a ghost known as solitude.

And of course, the promise I made to Shane. It was time to start looking for Sarah-Beth, but I battled with this reponsibility, dreaded the idea of it. If not for the love of my departed friend, I simply would have continued to drink with no true aim, for it was *all* I cared to do.

Perhaps a week after I moved into the inn, I decided to aim my goal around drinking, beginning at the pub near the boutique where we'd met the girls the night Shane fell in love. I went for a stroll through the Quarter. I didn't find the pub, so I went to another one and ordered a whiskey. Then another. Piss drunk after a useless day of searching, I stumbled back through the fire-lit city and came back upon my inn. On the walk, an idea came to me like a drunken charm when I remembered that I had walked Sarah-Beth's friend, Gwendolyn, home the night we'd met them. A thought clapped into my brain, to ask her, Gwendolyn, how to find Sarah-Beth.

Even waking the next afternoon, I remembered this plan fully, so I threw up, drank water, slid on my dirty clothes from the day before, and left to find her. I wanted to find her before sunset for I thought that a nighttime visit would give her the impression that my intentions were sexual. My only intention was to tell her the truth and to find her friend. My head ached throughout the walk, and there was an incessant pounding just above my neck which remained later into the afternoon. Breakfast was overdue, and I needed a whiskey soon.

I stumbled towards the river to retrace my steps from that first night. Onward towards the levee in the distance, a long and perfectly green mound beneath a blue early spring sky. It was about a mile to the river, and from there, I tripped along the banks until I came to the Quarter, which I walked through until I came to the church. I found the first pub that Shane and I had visited and gone inside. Nothing had changed. The young negro boy was still working behind the bar with the fat owner who was sweating through his shirt. The same stained wooden bar. The same dim yellow light from the candles. I only hoped that the bartender didn't remember who I was.

"How are you today, sir?"

"I'll have a whiskey," I said.

"You been in here before? You look familiar."

"No. Just the whiskey, please."

"You from around here?" He then placed a neat glass of whiskey before me, and I took a drink without acknowledging the question. Never removing my hand from the glass, I picked it up again and emptied it.

"No. Can I get another."

And another he poured, though not nearly as full as the first.

"You can fill it," I said. "I have money."

Through pondering eyes, he filled it nearly to the brim, then grabbed himself a glass and poured a small one for himself. He shot it back as I drank. I finished my second, then dug for my wallet. I pulled out a dollar and placed it on the bar while standing to leave.

"You don't want any change?"

"I don't care. Keep it," I said.

Even the sunlight's fading brightness ached my eyes after a short time in such a dark room. I walked back towards the church and turned right onto a street called St. Peter, then continued towards Bourbon, past several blocks to a street called Burgundy. The block looked familiar so I took a right. I walked for about five more minutes and eventually, I came upon a window that struck me with familiarity. I looked inside, and I was nearly certain that shop was the boutique where we'd met them. The pub next door, where we'd bought the girls their drinks, was closed.

From there, I stalked, unbalanced and wonderfully drunk and satisfied, back towards the river, as we had done with the girls, and tried to recall which way Gwendolyn and I had gone on the way to her place. Towards the direction of the barracks. I made a game of staying on the city blocks more challenging than you'd expect, and as I walked, I wandered across a creole man with a large iron fire staff, as he lit gas lamps that lined the streets. He carried a stool and placed it next to the lamp, stepped up with his iron lighter in hand, opened the small glass casing, and ignited the lamp with the flame. He moved downtown. I had sense enough of where the barracks were, even as walloping drunk as I was, so I went towards them, continuing until I reached the avenue called Esplanade. The oak trees that lined the road were draped with Spanish moss that multiplied in my vision, and the area appeared familiar. Across the way was a plantation mansion with large green hedges surrounding its perimeter. I'd seen the sight before and I knew how close I was. Up the next block, after a right, not forty meters later, her house with the red door loomed before me, grey and sinister in some odd way.

After all the walking, I began to feel sober. Sober enough. Too sober. This conversation with Gwendolyn was not one I wanted to have sober, but I fought with the idea of finding another drink nearby. Still, I was impatient and wanted the conversation to be over so that I could simply take the information and mull over it with a drink. I knocked four times. No one came for several seconds. Then, there was a sound behind the door that made me anxious. The door clicked open, and an older negro woman showed half of her face in the crack of the door, concerned eyes gazing through the slit.

"Yes?" She asked.

"Hello."

"What do you want here?"

"My name is Brady. Is there a girl named Gwendolyn who lives here?"

"She's not here."

"Oh, well, would you leave a message for me?"

"Who are you to her?"

"A friend, I suppose you'd call me."

"Would I now?"

"Acquaintance. I was hoping she'd help me find someone."

"Find who? For what reason?"

"What?"

"You heard me, boy. Why you need to find someone?"

"…Information."

"Why? You ain't no southerner. If you trying to find her father, you'll be in trouble. He's well protected."

"I'm not a northerner, and I'm only looking for Gwendolyn."

"What you want with her, boy?"

"Miss. I swear to you that you have no reason for suspicion. I just lost a dear friend to me in the war and I'm trying to find the woman he loved."

"Did Gwendolyn fall in love with a Yankee?"

"No. It wasn't Gwendolyn. It was a friend of hers. I swear it to you. I mean no harm."

The woman cracked the door a little wider. She was well dressed and her hair was pulled back. I could tell by the way she spoke that she was well-educated and intelligent. Her eyes were full of questions, and I felt that she understood me predicament.

"Listen to me," she said. "If Gwendolyn's daddy sees a Yankee standin' on his front stoop, he'll find a way to have you arrested if he don't kill you himself. You understand me?"

"Yes, ma'am."

"I'm trying to feel for you, but you're not safe here. And I smell the damn whiskey on your breath. You askin' for trouble even if you don't know it….Gwendolyn is downtown shoppin' on Canal Street. If not, she'll be on her way back. Maybe if you wait up on Esplanade, you'll run into her, but don't you dare let Mr. Thibodeaux catch you talkin' with that girl, you understand me? You'll get yourself killed."

"Yes, miss. Thank you."

"It's best you keep movin'. I'm sorry to hear about your friend. I really am. I can see it in your eyes."

I forced a weak smile and nodded. "Thanks," I said, turning to leave.

"Don't let a thing like that kill you, boy. Clean yourself up. I promise you, nobody wants you to die just because they did."

"You have a good night. Thank you for your help." I

turned my back and headed back towards Esplanade.

The avenue, covered by dirt, dust, and fallen leaves, crunchy from the winter, extended onward into the fading of the evening. There was a large strong oak in the neutral ground between the roads and I went to it and sat with my back up against the trunk. My skin felt grimy, my head chilly and damp. I closed my eyes and shortly after, fell asleep. It had been warm then, but when I woke up, there was a chilly breeze, and all the gas lamps down the sides of the road were then lit. I worried that I had slept through Gwendolyn's return. My head ached with something horrible, and I pined for whiskey.

She soon appeared on the opposite side of the road. How I'd forgotten how beautiful she was, her curly brown hair flowing gracefully across her shoulders. A man was walking with her and for a moment, I was even overcome with jealousy. Their voices came into earshot and I discerned that he was her father and the jealousy settled down. He was a tall man, his voice gruff and deep, and his accent unique, whimsical but stern, unlike any I'd heard before. All the words he spoke seemed to have the 'ah' or 'oh' sounds to them, but the sounds were elongated and nearly ridiculous. He was lumbering and threatening as the old woman had said, and I remembered Gwendolyn saying he was a politician in our first meeting. I wondered if she remembered me? I hoped she didn't because I had an idea.

They walked across the road and turned down their block. She's said something that'd made him laugh which distracted me as I tried to recall how to pronounce his name. Thib-oh-dough. Seemed wiser to listen to the old woman's warning, but his laugh, bolstering on the opposite side of the block showed me that he at least had some sense of humor within. I thought that perhaps I could charm him, face to face. I came out from behind the tree and slid my hands into my pockets to keep them from shaking out in the open. I needed whiskey desperately. I fiddled with the whistle in my pocket. Talking to them now was a poor decision, but was it the only opportunity? I took one more deep breath and called out to them.

"Excuse me! Sir, are you Mr. Thib-oh-dough."

Both of them turned to me, confused.

"Yes, it is. Who do I have the pleasure?"

"The name is Wayne," I said in my best southern accent. "John Wayne of Jackson, Mississippi. It's a high honor sir, for you see, I'm a new resident of Louisiana and I plan on voting for you in the next term."

He beamed a great big smile, reaching out a respectful hand to shake. "Well, the honor is all mine, Mr. Wayne. Afraid to say that I'm not so sure I'll be running, but time will tell. I suppose only time will tell."

Out of the corner of my eyes, I saw Gwendolyn peering at me with a confused familiarity.

"You're a proud Democrat then, are you?" Thibodeaux asked.

"Absolutely."

"When did you arrive in the city?"

"Only a few days ago. Why do you ask?"

"Well, are you finding all you need? Steady residence? Employment? You gotta job son?"

"Not quite. I've taken residence at an inn out towards Chalmette. The little bit of money I made in the service pays for me right now."

"Thank you for that service."

"There's no need, sir. The honor is all mine."

"Son, you served this country proud…And it's an outright shame that good men like you are going off and dying because weak politicians believe that this country should have open borders. Why do you think we can't get the advantage of the north? Don't believe the papers for a minute. We can't."

"The way I see it, sir, is that I had a duty, and regardless of what the powers that be think are best, I was going to serve my duty with diligence. And I did."

"This country needs more men like you, Mr. Wayne."

Gwendolyn continued to stare at me. Was it that she remembered my face?

"Forgive me for my bluntness, Mr. Wayne," Thibodeaux continued, "I understand it ain't popular to value yourself as a sentimental man, meanin' myself, but it downright breaks my heart, the way our country treats men like you. All of these filthy Irish and Italians flocking to New York and Boston, and the northern government puts their livelihoods and well being over proud American men like yourself. The very men fighting for this country. This government should be ashamed of itself."

"That's not necessary, sir."

"No, I mean it. In my opinion, if I might, this government has a duty to you, to send those filthy foreigners right back to where they came from, but you see, that doesn't suit the north's interest. Instead, they throw those same filthy foreigners in a uniform and send them down here to try and kill true men like you. American men. My great grandfather was born in this country, you know. He fought in the revolution, and I guarantee you, son, he didn't do it so that his predecessors would suit up and try to kill the same scum he'd already killed when we won this country. Why the damn northerners can't understand that outsiders killing our people is wrong is fully beyond me."

"As I said, sir. I just served my time. Whatever was to happen to me already has. Time to just move on to a new profession, I suppose."

"Well, Louisiana is lucky to have you."

"I sure wish you were right, sir. Hate to say so, but I think I've been enjoying New Orleans's offerings a bit too much."

"I wasn't going to say anything, myself, but boy, you reek of whiskey." He said this with a laugh and a friendly smack on the shoulder.

"Daddy," Gwendolyn said. "Enough. You're gonna embarrass Mr. Wayne."

"He's right," I replied. "Been drinkin' a fair amount."

"Son, if anyone deserves a drink, it's you. A man who fights in the war ain't gonna hear any guilt from me...and I'm a Christian. Enjoy yourself. God'll forgive ya....Hell, I should be embarrassed, Mr. Wayne. This is my daughter, Gwendolyn Thibodeaux."

"Charmed," I said. "Your father is a very wise man."

"Oh, she won't agree with you on that one, son."

"Stop it," she replied. "Don't say things like that. I've defended your opinions in public before."

"It appears that my baby girl is ready for her supper. You know how these women get when they're hungry. She's always hungry, John. Makes me think that perhaps with a small contribution, a little more than a service man's salary, that the two of you could have dinner…on my dollar, of course."

"Don't put this man on the spot, daddy," she said.

"Gwendolyn baby, he's put me on the spot. It's not often that a father comes across a man who he finds suitable for his baby girl. Maybe suitable ain't the word, but trustworthy. What do you say John…you care to have dinner with my girl?"

"Only with the lady's approval."

It was now clear in her eyes that she did remember who I was and that she wondered why I was back. She did not appear pleased.

"…I suppose we could," she said.

"Well wonderful," Mr. Thibodeaux said. "Tomorrow night then?"

"Does that work for you, Mr. Wayne?"

"Of course…I'll meet you here for eight."

"Eight? Great Christ, no. That's late, boy. Listen, we live just down the block right here, the little house with the red door. Be there at six and have her home by nine. Can we agree to that?"

"Sure, sir."

"Excellent. Good manners, like any great Democrat should have. John, it was a pleasure to meet you."

"You as well, Mr. Thibodeaux. Been a long time coming. Miss Gwendolyn, until tomorrow?"

"See you then, John."

I shook her father's hand, and started back towards the river. On my way, there on a quiet street corner, there was a small pub, lit by candlelight. I went in and ordered a whiskey.

"We ain't got any ice," the barkeep said.

"I don't care."

He poured a neat glass, and I drank.

I went ahead and drank myself piss drunk, finally leaving when the bartender there refused to serve me anymore. So I walked outside, but the thought of returning to the inn made me bored or sorrowful, I can't remember which. Perhaps both. The world spun a good deal, and it'd be tough to formulate a sentence. Slowly I had to accept the reality that ordering another drink, even at a different pub, was likely an impossibility. I went down to the river, and though the world around it spun, the river, she appeared still and beautiful. It was grand to acknowledge something was beautiful, something that demanded nothing in return. The river just flowed there, allowed dirty watchers like me to appreciate her beauty. She appeared so still. I approached her. I took a seat on the banks and stared out upon the water, the glimmers on her surface from the gas lamps that lined her by the road, awed by her and her beauty.

Ten

How or when I reached the inn that night before, or that next morning, I didn't know. When I woke, my body was dampened in sweat, my skin clammy and feverish, and when I woke, the nightmares faded away into oblivion. I recollected nothing. Not their stories. Not their meanings, whatever they were. The afternoon was already upon me, so I slipped on pants and went out to stand in the daylight to get a sense of what time it was. I suffered through a headache and some nausea and took a bath.

I drank some whiskey in the tub to kill the headache, and as slowly became drunk, I began to humor the idea of abandoning the war. The drunker I grew, the more this thought made me smile. The reason was pure and based solely on love. Why else would the fantasy come with such ease? I thought of how wonderful it would be to return to New York, to live with my mother and sister again. I could find myself once more, I thought and chuckled. Perhaps with them, it would feel normal to feel sober. Full of humor that morning, I was. Perhaps with them, I once again could take responsibility for something. I was unable as of late, and this only emphasized the point. I couldn't go back to the war now, and lead men. Going back, that was against the best interest of the country, for it wasn't that I wanted to drink. It was that I had to drink, and not without consequence. I'd found myself overtaken with this horrible state of depression, and hell, I doubted my ability to be responsible for anything so simple as eating a meal, much less leading soldiers. My fault, of course, but true non the less. I surely was more harmful than helpful to anyone.

In the mirror, I couldn't hide howm uch I began to look like my father, for this drinking to survive was the way of useless men. A man unequipped to handle responsibility. Purposeless. A burden in more ways than not. It seemed true that I was my father's son. It was.

Perhaps I was like my father in the way of lust as well, perhaps as much as his need for a drink. Lying there in that tub, I thought of Gwendolyn, her long curly brown hair, flowing over her collarbones, down to her bare chest. Her green eyes were full of daring anger. Christ, what a beautiful bitch of a woman. My mind could fill in the details of just how beautiful she was. Oh, the base, pure pleasure it brought me to think about her body. The curves in her breasts and her back. Those tense, strong calf muscles bare with nothing but my eyes to coat them. Her hateful mouth slipping into a smile of feminine ecstasy. I thought about what I could do to it, her body, and how little feeling it would take to do so. Pure, base, desire. The desire to be a beast, and to have a drink and smoke a cigarette after doing so without a passing glance.

I caught myself and told myself to drink more, for it seemed that in this sobriety, or only slight inebriation, that I ran the risk of losing my morality. I reminded myself to drink more. Drink until my thoughts were those of a good man again. So I did. I drank enough to curse myself for thinking such terrible thoughts. I had to do this for Shane. Not for myself and my desires. For Shane and the promise I made him.

The afternoon dripped by slowly like the residue of rain from gutters, but evening eventually crept upon me and I left early, around a quarter after four, to have a drink in town before dinner with Gwendolyn. I rolled a cigarette before I left and smoked it on my walk down to the river. The river in ways was even more seductive than the immodest thoughts of Gwendolyn, more fitting for what I deserved.

I came across a magnolia tree, one I hadn't noticed before on the many walks I'd taken down the river. It had the lovely beginning bloom of an early, warm March, partial not full. The contrast of green leaves and white peals were vibrant, gentle, and pure. I stopped for only a quick moment and sat underneath the tree, thought about the life it took from the brutal sun and the powerful, beautiful river which flowed through the soil and into the tree's roots, and for that short while, my mind was a peace.

Only minutes later, I stood and picked the bud of a magnolia for Gwendolyn, holding it gingerly in my palm for the rest of the walk.

When I arrived at her house, after two quick whiskeys at a local pub, I knocked twice on the red door, my consciousness dreary but joyful. The creole woman came to the door, damn near fainting at the sight of my face.

"Hello?"

"Hello…I've come for Miss Gwendolyn."

"Come for her?"

"Yes, miss. We've planned to have dinner together."

She stepped out of the house, closing the red door behind her. "You tryna get yourself killed?"

"There's no need for concern. I have spoken consent from her father."

"Does he knew where you come from?"

"Jackson, Mississippi."

"Don't lie to me boy. You may be able to get that nonsense past him, but not on me."

"We only need to talk."

"About what?"

"I told you only yesterday. She knows the woman who loved my friend."

"And that's why you're lookin' all cleaned up? Sure as hell cleaner than yesterday. I know how you servicemen think. Hell, all men. I've worked for men my whole life. You got that look in your eyes."

"What look, ma'am?"

"It's either hope or somethin' dirty."

"I assure you it's hope, and not for the reason you think."

"You gonna make that a promise?"

"Yes, miss."

"Don't you lay a finger on her, boy. You understand me?"

"Yes, ma'am."

"I don't like this one bit."

"I wish it could be something different."

She pierced me with her eyes and then turned and went into the house, leaving the door cracked. I heard her call, 'Well come in,' after a moment, so I did. It was cool inside, dark and well decorated with dollars, but lacking imagination. A large painting rested over the mantle of an old gentleman, pouting, miserable, and I assumed this was Mr. Thibodeaux's father. I imagined that if there was a painting of my father in my house, how it would destroy me slowly over time to look at his face day after day, and to feel shame at the sight of his drunken, oil painted eyes.

Gwendolyn finally came down the stairs, and though she was beautiful, she looked laden with the task before her. She wore a light blue spring gown that brought out the green in her eyes. My, she had terrific posture. Straight as a wooden plank, just like her personality. It was the best posture I'd ever seen, and I'd been around war generals for over a year. Puzzling how the people with the best posture struggle simply to smile.

"Hello...You look lovely," I said.

"Thank you. Where are we going?"

"I thought we'd find a nice place in the Quarter."

She and the creole woman shared a look, silently communicating negative judgments.

"I brought you this," I said, pulling the bud of the magnolia out of my pocket.

She looked down at it, puzzled, forcing a smile before taking it. "Thank you. Should we go?"

"Sure."

"Remember what I told you," the creole woman warned.

"Mrs. Harris. Be nice."

"Yes, ma'am," she replied.

She dropped her head, then opened the door wide for us.

As we walked, we kept a distance between each other, and we didn't walk far. She knew of a place only a couple blocks away. It was a small, empty cafe. I suggested a table by the window, but she went for a table near the rear of the restaurant. After a good while of silence, the waiter came by and gave us menus, though I wasn't hungry. I only wanted whiskey. She ordered a cup of chicken gumbo and a turkey sandwich on French bread, so I ordered the same.

"When did you come back?" she asked when the waiter had returned to the kitchen.

"You did know it was me then."

"I'm not stupid."

"You're not. That didn't take long."

"I could have had you arrested yesterday."

"Why didn't you then?"

"I wanted to know why, and I still do. I plan on being home by within the hour."

"I'll have you back by whenever you give me what I want."

"If my father knew who you were, or who you fought for, he would have you jailed in an instant."

"Well, thank you for sparing me, truly."

"Go on then. What do you want?"

"I've come to ask you a favor, okay."

"I can't help you."

"You don't even know what—"

"I'm not aiding someone from the north. It's that simple."

"I'm not your enemy. I promise that this has nothing to do with the war."

"Then what?"

"Do you remember my friend. The one you met on the river that night?"

"Yes. What about him?"

"He died in battle on the water."

A silence ensued, though it lasted only a short while, too

short in my opinion.

"I know which side he fought for as well."

"It isn't important."

"Of course it is."

"We're not fighting anymore."

"My father doesn't respect people who don't know what they're fighting for, and neither do I."

"I'm not here to please you, and I assure you that I'm not pursuing anything romantic."

"Then why are you here?"

"I need to know where to find your friend."

"What friend?"

"Sarah-Beth. She loved Shane."

"What do you want with her?"

"Shane loved her. They were betrothed when he died and she deserves to know. Is that enough for you?"

Gwendolyn grew quiet and for a moment, I felt there may have been a person living somewhere behind those daring, green eyes.

"Please," I said. "I don't know how I can find her without you."

"I already told you that I can't help you."

"Why?"

"Her safety."

"For Christ's sake. You know I mean her no harm. You know that."

"Why should I help you?"

"Does this have to be a negotiation? He was very dear to me, and his wishes are very dear to me. I promised him that I would come back and tell her, so just tell me where I can find her, and you'll never see me again. Honestly. I mean that."

"The South upholds its values without emotion, and you don't seem to understand that. I've shown a world of mercy just meeting with you today. I should have had you arrested last night."

"This isn't about sides. God! What's it going to take to

show you that? I'm desperate, ma'am, you hear that? I am drunk, desperate, and torn to fucken' pieces. I'm destroyed, that's what I am. I lost one of the only people in my life that means anything to me. Imagine how it feels to realize that the only good you're capable of is fulfilling their dying wishes before you die yourself, and if I can't do that, then I may as well be dead right now. Hell, it would be a damn relief to be dead."

"If you don't think this is about sides, perhaps that is the good you're capable of."

"What?"

"Your death. Your friend's death was necessary." She said this and her eyes went sharp and lifeless. Never have I wanted to slap a woman until that moment. I bit down on my tongue, bunching my fists tightly.

"Are those your thoughts or your fathers?"

"We share blood."

"Yes, yet somehow, I know that yours is far colder than his could ever be."

"We share blood."

"Well have a fucking crown then."

"I think this conversation is over."

"Shane and I were blood too. Irish Blood, not tied to the north or this bloody country in any way. We didn't ask to fight in your fucken war or be identified by our blood. And he certainly didn't ask to shed it for 'the north.' You hear. He didn't want to die in it. How stupid," I said, and for a moment, couldn't hold back laughter. "He loved a woman from the south, yet you in all your brilliance, still somehow consider him an enemy."

"Well, you can thank your Northern leaders then."

"No, I won't. I won't thank anyone, for this war is cruel and horrible, and in fact, the most horrible thing I've come across in my life, aside from maybe you."

"I'd like to leave now."

"I'd like nothing more, believe me, but I'm not leaving unless you tell me where she is."

"I will not for her protection."

"Perhaps it's your protection you should be worried about because I in no way wish to harm her."

"Are you threatening me?"

"I gain nothing from hurting her."

"I want to leave."

Impulsively, I took her wrist, gripping it tightly in my hand. "She deserves to know what happened."

"She won't be moved. I assure you, she didn't love him."

My eyes aimed at her life as my musket did that gaping wound across his chest. "You will never hurt me more than his death already has."

"She did not love him."

"And what would a woman like you know about love?" The fear was real and alive in her eyes now and I fed off of it. There was a steady whimper in her voice.

"She's my best friend, and you don't know anything about her."

"Then there's no harm in letting me talk to her." I gripped her wrist tighter. She squealed slightly, but I never loosened the grip. "Allow goodness to be the reason," I said. "What else do I have to lean on? I have no home. I know no-one. I have no friends, and I've been drinking since I've woken, and I will continue until I pass out tonight. I understand your hesitance, and your fear, I do…but I'm not a hurtful person. I'm simply hurting. Please, allow goodness to be the reason."
I let go of her wrist. She took in a breath.

"I won't be in New Orleans much longer," I said. "I promise, you won't see me again."

"If I see you again, you'll be locked up for the rest of your pathetic life."

"Fine. I'll say it again, I'm not your enemy, miss."

"You are."

"If it makes you feel any better, just know that I wish it had been me. I'd rather be dead, but now I can't die until his wish is fulfilled. I would never harm her, I promise you. I loved my friend too much."

"You harm her way of life. You harm our brothers and fathers for no other purpose than power and superiority."

"I have no power. Why would I even entertain such an idea? I moved from my country to escape famine, and before I even so much as had a meal on land, they had me on a ship, in a uniform. I have nothing but a promise to someone dead."

"You put on the wrong uniform."

"I didn't have a choice."

"You did. You always have a choice and you made yours, and men died because of it."

The stillness of the silence was deafening, and my anger grew with every second. I fought the image of that man with the scar, the man who killed Shane, for it was the only other time in my life I could remember being so angry. The anger felt to be bursting from my heart like a fresh scab being ripped from the skin. Oh, how I wanted to harm her. I wanted to see her die like that man. Her gorgeous green eyes may as well have been his scar being reopened, never to heal.

"Just tell me where I can find her. I'll find her regardless, I have to. Please," I said.

Her eyes softened. Perhaps my thoughts were animated in my eyes, or my will was clear, and my will to fight my emotions, more so.

"I hate this. I hate telling you this. We have lunch at the Pelican Club on Tuesdays at eleven. I'll show up late. She gets there at ten-thirty."

I took a calm breath for the first time since arriving, like a drowning mouth finally breaching the surface of the water.

"Thank you. God, thank you."

"Don't expect her to be moved. She won't be."

I had no comment. The waiter brought out the two bowls of gumbo and the turkey sandwiches. The food looked delicious but the thought of eating repulsed me. I felt sick. Looking at her hatched fantasies that struck me. Striking her, killing her, or worse. The meat just behind the bone of my forehead craved the feeling whiskey would soon give it. "I have to go," I said. "Give your father my gratitude for the meal."

And I stood to leave without a word or glance, and in one moment, I understood my father slightly more. I understood how we were connected, and while that thought repulsed me, for once I remained with it. I walked, and as my thoughts calmed, that depressive emptiness began to overtake me again, seeping through my body like molasses. Self-doubt. Darkness. My head throbbed as though it was already drunk. I stopped at a pub and drank three quickly, and they churned like a symphony in my brain. They brought me calm thoughts, lightness, and comfort, and satisfaction in being alone. Hope with no action, and it was sweet and just what I needed.

I walked back to the inn. When I went inside the room, it seemed more quiet than usual. Then the stillness of guilt amplified. Or perhaps it was the guilt itself that was quiet. Guilt is quiet because it mutes every other feeling around it.

Eleven

I'd meet with Sarah-Beth three days into the uncertain future, and uncertain because, other than the future event itself, there was little to hope for, or live for. There were many baths and many bottles. Each afternoon when I woke, one grand and looming thought rang true in my head incessantly and unrelenting. The thought that Shane had been the lucky one.

When the inevitable thought came, I'd go and sit on the banks of the river. This was hardly active, as if she called me to her. That by some mysterious power, she appeared as the only remedy for this ache. The power in her flow intoxicated me, and I felt such power just by standing on her banks.

It was only Saturday, and Tuesday was the faithful day. I woke to sip down a couple fair glugs of whiskey, a partial remedy, then staggered out of the inn towards the great river, drawn by the ornamental glow of her white shimmers in the daylight. I stared into the deceptively still water and filled my brain bright with images of taking a swim. Oh, true I was lonely and grieving, but a swim would unify me with the others she'd taken. This was not my home, but if any place were to be called such, it was her. Hours passed and she grew into a kind of fantasy. I even avoided throwing an empty bottle into her, chucking it behind me instead. And I thanked her, just for being there and beautiful.

She assured me that I deserved to be with her. In good faith, she needed me, and therefore, how else did I free myself than by deciding that my tenure in the war must end. The thought, of course, was a recalling of a past idea, but now with a spine. With a true reason. So down the river, I walked, nearly unable to pull my gaze away from her for the entire trail to the barracks where I hoped Captain Harrison was.

Inside the barracks, their faces were blurred now, and I gave an affront when I heard my own name, Brady, repeated to me with concern. They were now men of no identity in my mind, even if once I knew them. As I meandered past them, through the reeking hallways, some smiled. Others didn't. Those who greeted me, I fended off with a smile and a nod.

There, not far off, turning after using the latrine, I saw his dark black curls from behind, unprepared for the red wave of hatred that came to me and struck me even more violently when Benjamin turned around and his eyes met with my own. There did it boil between us, the anger. The certainty that I was capable of his end. Though such a thought was not my purpose. I thought of the river, and it calmed me, long enough at least that his eyes turned away and he continued to walk on his merry way. It ached me so to think that with a simple swing of luck, it could have been him and not my friend. How unjust it seemed that God, whatever that was, seemed to have a purpose for someone so useless, yet such a firm, quick death for someone so loved. How was it possible, for it certainly wasn't fair, and perhaps the most reprehensible case of religeous injustice.

I continued on to a row of office doorways for captains and generals. There on the third door on my right was a door with a plaque that read NAVY captain. I knocked, and that familiar, gruff, near fatherly voice, said, "Come in." Slowly, I opened the door. Showed my drunken face with a sudden veil of shame. He sat behind a desk, and it was odd to see him so relaxed.

"Brady."

"Hello, Captain."

"How are you, son? Getting by alright on your leave?"

"Getting by."

"Good. I'm glad you stopped by. I can fill you in on our progress. It appears that the Empire will be ready to sail a little sooner than expected. There was plenty of damage to her hull, but surprisingly little anywhere else. We plan to take her up to Memphis beginning Friday, so here's to say, I'll need you to report back to your post by then, and sooner preferably."

"That's why I'm here, Captain."

"Reporting today then, are you?"

"I'm afraid not."

"Well, by Thursday then."

"I hoped not."

"—What are you saying, son?"

"I'm saying that with your permission, I wish to be granted full dismissal."

"Hmm. Do you mean that?"

"I do."

"Well, I'm afraid I can't. It's out of the question, and be it known that on Thursday, you're to report to your post, under an order, as the Junior Lieutenant of this crew."

I bit my lip, looked above, and past his stern emotionless glance. "Captain. Don't misunderstand. I am grateful for the position, truly I am. But I'm. Uh. I don't quite know the word. I'm not good, and I don't think I can return to the war."

"Well, as understandable as that is, the fact is that you haven't been granted permission to leave your post, and therefore, if you do, it is desertion. We'd have no choice by to try you by a court-martial for a punishment that they see fit. But be assured from an insider, the punishment is death."

"I. Umm. I see."

"I'm glad to make it clear for you. Is there anything else I can answer?"

"What's the possibility that one could find mercy in a particular circumstance?"

"One which concludes in desertion?"

"Hypothetically."

"I'd be certain from your perspective that there would be zero tolerance. Knowing that, I think we can drop the subject."

"—Captain. I'm not capable of the post. You know I'm not."

"Oh son, you see, I'm certain of the contrary. I do think you're capable, even grieved as you are. And this may be a bit of personal bias, but I think forcing yourself to move on from this particular darkness you're facing, despite your hesitance to do so, may even be a good thing for you."

"I don't agree. I don't."

"Well, unfortunately for you, you have a very tough decision to make then. I can't say much more. You're ordered back to duty on Thursday. That's where I stand, and my word is final."

"I beg of you to reconsider."

His gaze turned back to me, dark and serious. He approached, never letting his gaze wander away from my eyes. "Stand up straight, damn it. Straight. Now there ain't nothing in the law that forbids a man to beg, but I warn you, Brady, don't make me regret my own decision. I've honored myself in my ability to judge character. To see the strength in the men I lead, to make them better men. And they're not all good men, I know that right well but know for certain that I would never promote a beggar to lead not only my men but his own, for a beggar on my crew is no honorable man. The sheer act of begging requires a man to put himself before others solely for his own purposes, and that's all fine and good, but it's not you. You've got wits about you, Brady. You're damn smart and competent, and to see you fall into a pit so deep over such a short amount of time is nothing short of a tragedy, but I wouldn't have promoted you unless I knew that you had it in you to pull yourself out. Well, the time has come, son. Now step out of my office. I don't much care for the sight of you right now."

There I turned to walk away, my soul moved however mild. Who did I kid? What did it change?

"Brady. I expect to see you Thursday at eight hundred hours. You're aware of my expectations."

"Yes, sir."

"Go clean yourself up, son."

Without the guts to show it, I walked out silently cursing him. He was no better than the others, for, like all men, he needed something. He needed a man to fight his battle. And while that is all fine and good, who would fight my own. How simple it was to say return by this day, at this place, at this hour, regardless of what you need. Return because I need you here. I didn't need them. I didn't need the crew, or the ship, or the cursed war. I needed my family. No, I needed to find Sarah-Beth, and I needed the river. The sunset behind her before I made it back, for I'd taken my time in stopping for a drink, and then gazed upon the river. She glowed in the moonlight. Those small ripples that spread infinitely across her surface reminded me deeply of the bigger waves that always seemed to accompany Shane and the notes he played. It was as though looking through a mirror to see the memory of him shining through in some imaginary haven under the surface. Down there was an alien world where even a man as devastated as I was could find peace in both the past and the...well, if it even could be called the future? For that dear, horrible time, the river which was still there every morning, every evening, whenever I needed her, was there and ready for me. What else prevented me from giving myself up to her power than that fragile promise itself. I must find Sarah-Beth first. This battle reined on.

When I woke on Monday, the sunset was mere hours away. I went out to the pump and sucked down water with a parched and acrid mouth, drinking so quickly that I gasped for breath. My head went on throbbing and aching, even after hydrating, so I began to drink whiskey again to ease this pain. I gulped down four swigs before I gagged. After a second of recovery, I stomached four more. I started to sweat, and my body began to itch. I wondered when was the last time I cleaned my clothes.

Outside, it was a beautiful spring afternoon, and I stepped out into the breeze. The relief of the coolness was heavenly, and I spread my arms and closed my eyes. I imagined Jesus, and it made me laugh. Yes, to imagine Jesus, robe and all, standing in a brothel in New Orleans. I laughed and how very drunk

I was. I belched and some whiskey came up. It struck me that I was holding an empty bottle so I gave it a nice throw across the field. Then I went back inside to open the fresh bottle and picked up my pail to fill it with water so that I could have a bath before my swim. The weather was so heavenly, so I flipped the pale upside down, took a seat, and drank alone for a couple of minutes. I'd save this whiskey for the swim. Just a quick swim. It would be good exercise that I hadn't had in a while. Great exercise. I filled the bucket with water and brought it back inside into the washroom. The pale was heavy, and without thinking, I dropped the bottle of whiskey on the floor where it shattered. The brown alcohol pooled between the sharp shards of green glass.

I laughed. "No," I said, loudly, laughing again. "No, it can't be true." I stared at it as though I myself were a match about to be dropped on a bail of hay. "It's time. It must just be time."

My skin was oily, I was clammy and I wanted my bath, but the sunset was close, and soon enough, the cool water of the lovely Mississippi would give me that refreshing satisfaction I so desired. The cool water would clean that clamminess away.

When I was a young boy, Shane and I would find and jump in large muddy puddles after heavy rain. We'd gather big wads of mud with our hands and throw them at each other, and come back with faces and clothes saturated in the mud. Our mothers always faked anger in front of us, but then laughed to themselves when we bathed. "How did you get so filthy?" It always brought me joy to hear this question.

I smoked a cigarette in the inn room and filled it with a dry cloud. I jumped on the bed and howled until beads of sweat started dripping from my forehead and down my back. I imagined the river, and how it would finally feel to submerge my head below the water. The coldness surrounding my skin, and the satisfying pull of her current. I stopped jumping when my stomach grew queasy, and there was a slight burn in my throat. I vomited, there on the bed, a near gallon of whiskey. Then the room began to turn, speeding rapidly, so I stepped down off the bed and laid on the floor, watching the ceiling turn above my head. I stayed there for a few minutes, then with any will power left, I lifted myself. I struggled to slip my leg into my pants. The horrible thoughts started coming back rapidly now. I wanted the river's image. Not Shane. Not my father. The river. I forced my boots on roughly without socks, and there were hardened clumps of dried dirt between my toes, like fragile rocks. They were painful against my feet as I took steps towards the door. I stumbled out into the sunlight for sunset hadn't yet come.

The vast blueness of the sky was overwhelming. I walked out towards the river, over a mound of soft, green grass, stepping hard, trying to break the tiny clumps of dirt dancing in my shoes.

When I reached the bank, some people were standing by the river. They didn't matter to me, but I didn't want an audience. I walked away from the city. The past shimmered off the river, when usually she was so beautiful. I saw my father, and his boat, and the river Shannon, and these thoughts made me angry. *Not now.* This moment was mine, not his. He hadn't earned it. I hoped that where ever I went after death, if I went anywhere, that I wouldn't be there in the past with him. I hoped, prayed even, that he was somewhere else. I imagine the sight of his face, staring at me to see a spitting image of himself. His son. And was he proud, or disappointed like I was?

The small patch of green before the river leads to a pile of large and sharp rocks. I climbed over them, carefully, and finally came to one resting flat, close enough to the river to jump from. I crouched down on it and took a hard look at the godly river. I reached out and dipped a finger into her. Unnaturally cool she seemed. The translucent brown surface with a riotous charm underneath, her deadly current ready to take me.

Then it struck me that she was a killer and whether a peaceful killer was a mystery. I sensed she was a killer in my chest. I even felt the lives she'd already taken, and done so without a passing thought. She was haunting and ruthless. I felt them, the dead. I felt them as a collective and they were not at peace, for they were remembered by no-one, and they were resentful because of this. They felt cheated and betrayed. I felt their longing. Their regrets. Their notions that they were ending somewhere peaceful, only to realize this was a lie as their lives on earth had been. Somewhere peaceful like the sea, for the sea was order. She, this horrible river, chaotic. The worst man on earth hardly deserved her fate.

"Don't do it," spoke a voice from behind me. "You don't have to do this."

I turned to look behind me, and my eyes began to itch with tears, blurring my vision to who was speaking. I wanted them to see me, whoever they were. I yearned someone to please see me and the pain I carried. An older man, he was. He had bad posture. He wore a seersucker suit and leaned on a cane. His words were clear, and for some reason I trusted him.

"Come on back, son. You're young and capable, and it's not going to be like this forever. Come on back and give yourself a chance."

A rush of sadness shot up my gut into my throat like a train speeding down a rail. A sob pushed out of me from shame. I turned a gave the river another look and she was disgusted and stern. The attachement to her vanished. The dead remained dead, and I remained living crouched there on that rock.

"You're going to make it through this, now. Come on back," The pitch in his voice, charmed by his southern accent, was bright, almost colorfully humorous. In it, his voice, was extraordinarily calm, without worry or panic. He reached out as far as he could without climbing on the rocks, but the attempt was willful. I climbed back towards him.

"That's it. Come on. You're going to see tomorrow, son." He grunted as he lifted his cane from the ground and reached it out to me, his back in clear pain. I took a light grip on it and stepped back on the grass, still sobbing. The old man touched my shoulder and said, "Go home. It'll get better. Go on home."

Involuntarily it seemed that I embraced him, placing my head into his shoulder. I squeezed his frail body tightly in my arms like he was the father I never had. "I don't have one," I cried.

"It's alright."

"I don't have a home."

"You'll find one. It'll be alright."

His arms were warm and held me. He hugged me back, tightly as he could. "It'll be alright," he repeated. "You're gonna be alright."

And there, pushing my wet eyes and muted sobs into his shoulder, he patted the back of my head. And I let go, for just to hear another person say it'll be okay gutted me with its power. I'll be okay, even though he's gone. It'll be different, but you'll be okay. And what you find about peace, when you do find it, is that no cowardice lives there. Fear gives it that illusion, but there's only courage and goodness there.

The old man walked with me to the inn, speaking only of how it would be okay.

Twelve

Through the window, it was grey and ghostly, the rain falling in loads, and the sound of the water pattered the soft muddied ground, drumming the springtime leaves that floated on puddles, and they echoed and clapped in the water. I watched the water drench the town, and rested my aching forehead on the cool window. It was Tuesday.

At nearly ten, I jumped up in a rush. Sarah-Beth would be arriving at the Pelican Club soon and there was no time to bathe. No time to clean the bile and vomit off the floor or my clothes. I changed into a shirt less sullied, and blessed the rain for the cleaning I hoped it'd accomplish. My head pounded.

Traveling through the rain brought on a serene, healing quality. The cool fat drops fell on my head and liberated my spirit momentarily. The soothing pattering of water or the cool relief of otherwise red and burning skin. The Quarter soon came into my sight. I wondered if Gwendolyn had mentioned anything and if Sarah-Beth even knew that I was coming.

I'd seen her eyes the night they'd met. I'd seen his depression when they fell apart. I knew they loved each other if I knew nothing else. This was about them and no-one else.

By the time I reached the club, the rain had died to a light drizzle. My clothes were soaked, and there were several questionable gazes thrown my way as I walked in. I approached the maître d' and asked him if Ms. Sarah-Beth had arrived for her Tuesday lunch, and quickly he asked if I was her porter. I told him I was and that my message was urgent, and he had me wait at the podium while he went off to retrieve her.

She saw me as she moved forward from the back of the

restaurant and I saw in her eyes a coy, maybe even frightened smile that she recognized me. She started to approach. I was amazed to see her. I'd done it, and I thought of how Shane would have felt, seeing her face, how much joy it would have brought him. There was a deep curl of sadness in her glistening eye. She was indeed beautiful.

"Do you remember me?" I asked. I wondered how unsightly my appearance looked.

"I do," she said, pity alive in her eyes, which I assumed of my unsightly appearance. "You're Brady."

"It's so good to see you." Emotion rushed across me like a sheet of heavy rain on a lake. "I don't even know what to say. It's so nice to see you. How are you, truly?"

"I'm well, Brady," she said, and she smiled. "I don't mean to sound so blunt, but why are you here?"

"Of course. I have news…Do you think that we could step outside."

"Sure…There's a covered patio in the alleyway. We can go out there.

So we walked out, and I followed her to the back alleyway. Outside, the rain had reduced to a drizzle, and the sun had remained away, so the weather was grey and cool and breezy. Birds were chirping happily after baths.

"Is the ship back already?"

"It is. It's been back a couple of weeks now."

"A couple of weeks? Really?"

"Yes. Yes, it has."

"Where's Shane? If he's back, I should speak with him."

"That's why I'm here. Sarah-Beth. I don't know how else to say it. Shane's gone. He didn't make it from battle."

His fingers were flat and held tightly together as she brought them to her mouth. Her eyes went wide. She was silent.

The words struggled to come to me. "I—I promised him. I promised him that I'd come back to tell you. Tell you that he loved you. You maybe will never even know how much he loved you, but he did. I'm so sorry."

Her eyes squinted and dampened and she turned away from me to wipe them with the back of her hand.

"This. Oh, God. I'm sorry. This wasn't a conversation I was prepared to have today."

"How could you be prepared for something like that?"

"That's horrible, Brady. That's so horrible."

"But he loved you," I said, trying to smile through a reddened face. "That's means something. It makes it worth telling you."

She went silent again, thinking it seemed. "Thank you. Believe me. He loved you too."

"I know," I said, smiling, trying to share tears with her. "He was my best friend."

She brought her hand back up to her mouth, and with her flat fingers on her cheeks, I saw her left hand. It glimmered there on her finger. "I know he was. Thank you for telling me, and I'm so sorry for your loss."

"Is that a ring?" I asked.

"I beg your pardon?"

"That ring on your finger?"

She brought her hand away from her face and looked down at it, as though it were a surprise. "Oh."

"Did Shane give that to you?"

"I—Brady, listen."

"Is that ring from Shane?"

"Brady...I know this couldn't have been easy coming down here to tell me. It's very brave, so I feel like I owe you the same level of honesty."

"What is this...this ring?"

"Brady—"

"It's not from him?"

"No."

"Oh, piss off."

"Brady."

"Are you—engaged?"

"—Yes."

"To who?"

"To a man named Thomas."

"No," I said, shaking my head. "No, you're not. How could you be if you loved him?"

"I am, Brady."

"But how? How could you be engaged if you didn't know that Shane was dead? You wouldn't have done that—not if you loved him."

"I never said I didn't love him."

"Then how?!" I shouted. "It wasn't a long time. It was no time."

"Brady, I want a family. Children."

"He thought about you every day at sea. Every day! He was dreaming of the day he could come back to be with you."

"I never thought I'd see him again."

"Well, you were right."

"Brady—"

"He loved you!"

"That doesn't mean I didn't love him."

"Did you?"

"Did I what?"

"Did you love him?"

And there she went silent as death. She covered her truth with a face of false sorrow. My heart had fallen into my toes.

"I can't believe this," was all I could say.

"I'm sorry."

"Sorry for what?"

"For all of it. The whole of it."

"Wonderful. Well piss off and be sorry for yourself. It's clear that's all you give a damn about, you fucken' treasure."

"It never would have worked."

"Those are words he never would have said," I said, then muttered, "harlot," beneath my breath.

She gasped. "You're upset...I understand, but do not—"

"Yes, I'm upset! You betrayed him."

"I did not."

"For Christ's sake, you did. You did and he was ready to give you everything."

"It was never supposed to be this way."

"He wanted to be with you."

"I know that."

"So why? Tell me why he didn't deserve it?"

"He did! He did, Brady but it wasn't the right time."

"It was the only time! It was all the time he had and he was willing to give all of it to you."

"I couldn't stop living because he was trapped! That's just the way it was."

A man suddenly approached us. "Excuse me," he said. He was a squirrel of a man. His eyes were magnified through his rounded glasses, his face protected only by his white, curly mustache. He put his index finger up at me, though he was still some distance between Sarah-Beth and myself. "Is everything okay here, ma'am?"

"I'm fine, thank you."

"That's no way for a gentleman to speak to a woman," he said.

Rage rushed up to my spine to the base of my neck. "This doesn't concern you." He took this as a cue to come closer.

"I believe it does sir."

"Really? What gave you that impression."

"We gentleman have a responsibility to preserve in treating our women with respect and dignity."

"Right, even when they have none for anyone else," I said, directing the last part in her direction.

"Let's talk to the woman with some respect, yes?" He then touched my shoulder. I pulled it away from his hand on impulse, and on that same impulse, pushed him in the chest with my right hand. He fell backward, and when he looked up from the ground, shock lived in his eyes.

"Are you an animal?" he asked. I said nothing and stood over him, staring down. He stood. "I'm getting the authorities."

Sarah-Beth was frightened.

"You didn't deserve him," I said. "You never deserved him."

"There, then. You're right. Now please, leave."

"Are you not remorseful?" The door to the club slammed shut as the man had run in to to get the authorities.

"Enough of this."

"You monster. He was a good man."

"That's enough! Leave, now. Brady, please leave."

"Cast me away then. I'm not a burden to bear."

"I'm sorry about your friend. I'm sorry if I've hurt him or you…I really am, but I have to go." She started back inside.

"Run from it then! Go on and run back to your happy life."

"That man was right, you know. What a way to talk to a woman."

She walked back into the white room where she would sit and eat in warmth and peace, away from the coldness. Away from anything she deemed unimportant, she and all the rest inside the walls of the white room. Meanwhile, I stood outside, a vessel of a man, depleted like the empty chamber of a gun. I walked out of the gate leading back to the street and walked back towards the inn, and the rain began to fall again. I went to collect my things. I'd found her. My duty was done, and I had no reason longer to be there in New Orleans. I was certain of that. I wasn't certain, however, that I truly belonged anywhere.

Part Three

Her

Thirteen

"T'was on one bright March morning, I bid New Orleans adieu."
-The Lakes of Pontchartrain

It was Thursday. The morning was bright and warm, a late day in March, and I woke feeling well-rested for the first time in many weeks. I dressed in rinsed clothes that had dried overnight, made the bed, packed the few items I had, and drank some water. After a look upon the lonely room of the inn and I bid it adieu.

I took a long and thoughtful stroll to the train station and there was some hope on my mind. I hoped that I could settle my pain and leave it behind, in the swamps and muck where it belonged, here in this wet mush of land. There were parts of the city that any man would admire, the beauty of it that is. The mosses draped high on old oaks, and cypress trees, magnolia buds, and even the friendly air of the strangers, so long as you met them without ever getting to know them. It was impossible to deny that it was a beautiful place in its own mysterious way, with a sort of magic that floated through the narrow streets. Although, it's few bourgeois and aristocrats soaked and sweated and smothered the town with their own false sense of importance, giving it a self-righteous stink when around such a crowd. Boy, was it good to leave them behind, the dainty rich. It was a nice and temperate walk. A quick and well-deserved farewell.

The outside of the train station bustled. Men going to the war.

Women and children fleeing it. People escaping west for new opportunities. So many new and different paths started here in this stuffy, hot wooden terminal, where they waited with strangers who were neither enemies nor friends, and parted to the next phase of their lives, their reasons purely their own. I was going back to New York, and the thought that I would see my mother and sister in only a few days engorged me with new hope. I wondered how they were. I wondered if they thought that I was dead and imagined their faces once they'd discovered that I wasn't. Their reactions, crystal clear in my imagination, brought me overwhelming joy. And this joy diverted me from my fears. That I could be killed. That I could be caught and tried for abandoning my post.

Truly the decision came down to this purest simplicity. Go back to the war to die, either by their hands or my own, or attempt to find the ones I loved again, and risk dying in the process. Once conceptualized, the answer was only so simple. Death loomed regardless.

I stood in line at the ticket window and then asked the clerk for a map. The paper was yellowed for the map had been used, but the routes were clear enough. I would take a train north to Jackson, Mississippi, and then continue up to Grenada and up further to Grand Junction, Tennessee. Then I'd go east through Corinth, Decatur, then north again, until I reached Lynchburg, Virginia. From there, I'd hop another northbound train to Alexandria, cross over the Potomac into Washington, then travel upward to Baltimore, where I could take a train to Philadelphia. From there could I board a train for New York City. I feared my funds were too low but decided I would get as far as I could, then continue on foot, or by a miracle, until I found Manhattan. I stepped back in line and when I reached the ticket window again I asked the clerk for a ticket to Jackson.

"First class or coach?"

"Coach, please."

"That'll be eighty-three cents."

I slowly pulled the coin purse from my bag, then dug around, finding a half dollar and four dimes and I placed them on the counter. He slid them over to himself with his fingers, then stared down at them.

"This currenc, it ain't valid." He dropped it back on the counter. "Next in line please." The person behind me stepped up, but I blocked them from the window with my body.

"What do you mean?" I asked.

"I mean I ain't takin' this money."

"Why not?"

"This ain't the currency I'm lookin' for. This here's Union currency."

"It says United States on it."

"I ain't takin' Union currency," he said in a mumble. "It's that simple."

"You are aware that New Orleans is a Union city?"

He leaned inward, gave me a gesture with his fingers. "Not here, it ain't," he whispered.

He slid the handful of coins back into his palm, looked me in the eye, then tossed them back through the window where they hit me in the chest and rained to the floor about my shoes. I managed to keep a level head about myself, though I delighted in the image of hitting him in the mouth. I leaned down and picked up the money, then stood, taking a deep breath, holding together the calmest disposition.

"One ticket to Jackson," I said.

"Fraid I can't do that."

"Listen. I have family up north. My mother and my sister need to be taken care of and I have not seen them for a very long time."

"Fighting in the war, I take it?"

"Yes, and it's been a hell of a time. Allow me to go see them. I ask with all of the respect I have."

"Shame to hear it, but you see, your funds are insufficient, therefore, I gotta insist that you get that ugly maw of yours outta ma window, you understand?"

"Please, sir. I beg of you."

"I don't give a damn. Step outta ma line."

"It's no problem if you just allow me a bloody ticket on the train!"

He smiled. "The day I allow some nigger lovin' Yankee on this train...well, that's the day I myself will be one, and boy... that day ain't never gonna come."

"What are you playing at you right prick!"

"Stop...right there," he said, he held the small barrel of the revolver low, out of sight to the other passengers.

"I'm a man with a family for the love of Christ. I'm not a Yankee."

"I don't give a shit if you're Joan of Arc. You'd die just as quick. Now whatever non-sense, you've been through, it ain't none of my concern, so why don't you step aside so these good people behind you can get to where they goin'."

Even though the glass, I heard the revolver cock.

"Last warning, nigger lover."

Suddenly then, two hands gripped my shoulders and pulled me backward with force. When I turned to see who it was, I was met with a bundled fist in my jaw. I came down on my palms to keep my face from hitting the floor, right dazed. Then came a kick in my guy amidst shouts of 'nigger lover'. Five men had joined in on the mobbing, and eventually, I found some ground under my toes, pushed myself up, and ran, getting a solid clock on the back of the skull before I fled. They didn't chase me. They seemed content with only a light beating. Women screamed as I ran.

The pain didn't start to take until I was outside, assured for the moment that I was safe. It was still bright and temperate. I held my jaw as I walked and was beginning to feel the bruising on my head and back. I found a clearing where I took a seat and pulled out the map and my compass. The map showed that the northbound train to Jackson started west before turning north, and I knew there would be cargo cars bringing aid to the troops in the north. I thought that if I could sneak aboard one, I could move in the right direction. Despite the hope in the idea, I knew that the confederate dangers only increased the further away from New Orleans I went. Hell, the confederate dangers were here. I only imagined the hell I'd face in Mississippi and beyond. I knew that I couldn't stay in New Orleans though, for if I did, I was just as much a danger to myself. Perhaps I'd get lucky and find a cargo car filled with unsuspecting uniforms, something I could disguise myself in.

My best bet was to try and board the train as it was moving out, and find a hiding place while the train was in motion when all would be inside the passenger cars. I walked west, past the station until the tracks were in the clear. Then I walked along the tracks a little over a mile. I came to a tree on side of the tracks and I sat down, leaning my sore back against the trunk. I rolled a cigarette and smoked while I waited. I craved whiskey, and I was hungry for I hadn't eaten since the previous morning. I was very hungry. I sat there with nothing but time ahead of me.

More than half an hour passed before I heard the bellow of the locomotive in the distance. I shouldered my bag, moved over to the opposite side of the tree trunk to hide myself. The horn bellowed again. The locomotive came around the bend, moving slowly, but gaining speed, the hopper car behind it, filled with coal, then came the cargo. My time was short. It gained speed as my breathing did, and as my heartbeat did. *'To a stolen bottle in Jackson tonight'* The horn bellowed again, echoing through the bright blue sky, and when the locomotive passed the tree, I began to run, weight bouncing in my bruises.

It was moving faster than I had thought. The hopper car raced by me and I picked up my speed, my bag painfully bouncing on my back with each stride. I looked back to see if there was any cargo car with an open door. There wasn't. It was the sixth or seventh car, that had a half-cracked open roof hatch, and that was one I'd have to take. I slowed slightly to let the car come to me. My body cramped with soreness and my chest burned with little breath. I focused on the iron ladder on the side of the seventh car, and tried to rid my mind of how gruesome my death would be if I were to miss with just one simple slip of my foot. The ladder came to my side and I took in a gasp of air and reached out towards it. I aimed for the third rung, leading with my right foot, and jumped. I gripped hard on the rail and my foot came down on the third rung, but I lost my footing and my left foot fell, my shin knocking against the iron. The pressure moved over to my arms, back, and right leg. I felt it all the way in my chest in a painful heave as though I had caught the train itself. But I held tightly, bringing my left leg back unto the rung, and made the short climb onto the platform between cars. I was on, moving with the train, watching the land of Louisiana move past me with gathering speed. I sucked in air, trying to catch my breath. Then I began to club the roof of the car. Once on top, I pulled up and looked down into the hatch, unable to see anything but a dark abyss below, and I put my legs in one at a time, holding tightly to the ledge, then let go. I fell in and landed hard inside the rattling darkness.

<h1 style="text-align:center">Fourteen</h1>

I hoped the ankle was only sprained, but the pain felt sharp and agonizing. I had come down on the corner of an empty wooden crate which flipped over, rolling my ankle on the floorboard. Even if it were only sprained, I knew from that moment, the injury would be debilitating. A small beam of sunlight gleamed through the half-opened hatch and dust specks floated on the light's edge onto a large crate that rested under the beam, and this was the only light inside the car. I pushed myself forward, through the junk and storage inside the car, with my good ankle, avoiding any pressure on the other until I found a hiding space. The car rattled, clunking harshly on the tracks. Occasionally, the horn bellowed.

The train moved along for about an hour. Then suddenly, a crate behind me jutted forwards as the train began to break, slowing and eventually squeaking to a stop. All was eerily quiet after that and all I heard was my own nevous breath between the silence, as I wondered if they knew I was aboard.

A half-muted clunk came from the next car over. Then I heard a man's footsteps ring out on the iron of the platform between the cars. He banged on the door of the cargo unit and the bang rang through the metal, so hard I could feel its vibration. All went quiet again. I tried to quiet my breathing and hoped that if they came inside that the sounds of my own heartbeat wouldn't give me away. The dusty beam of light then grew as the roof hatch opened wide. A shadow of a head in silhouette came into the light on the floor of the car. "Give yourself up," he said. His tone was a matter of face, serious but non-threatening. "Hello? We know you're down there. Come on out."

For a moment, I considered it. I was tightly packed behind the crate, my breath held, my swolen ankle throbbing. A compacted kind of hell, it was. I took in hefty gasps of air into my nose, my chest rising with sound.

"Don't make me open the door. You're just slowing everyone down. Come on out," he called from above. I remained still, and eventually, I heard him sigh in defeat. "Alright."

The hatch above slammed closed and completely enveloped me in darkness. I listened intently for the sound of him climbing back down the latter. Then I heard the clunking latch being undone. Metal pulled and slammed. I was still packed tightly behind the crate, still in darkness when the door slid open and light rushed in. My heart raced. My ankle pounded as though my heart had been relocated. My hands trembled, and fear embraced me like loneliness does a drunk.

I heard him climb aboard, sure he was attemptin' to keep quiet. Suppose his frustration got the best of him, for he then flung a wooden crate which crashed onto something hard, the wood crackin in the mess of crap. I flipped over onto my stomach and began to crawl between the cargo, no plan as to my escape.

"This is getting to be a real pain in the ass," he said. I saw his shadow moving on the wall behind me. "Don't make me mad now, boy, come on now." I stayed crouched, quietly moving, trying not to slide my clothes against the floor. Then he pushed another crate and one of its sharp corners came down squarely on my temple. I bit my lip to keep from howling in pain. That sucker right hurt, even more than the ankle in the moment. I pushed my palm hard against my head and squinted my face tightly, using the other hand to cover my mouth, biting down on my lip.

"I know you're in here. They done caught you jumping the train back in New Orleans. They just wasn't gonna stop over the lake. If you come out, we'll let you keep your due process. This ain't a bad deal."

I didn't like my chances in a court of law. I was an Irishman and if they found out I was a deserting junior lieutenant, as if they wouldn't want to kill an Irishman just for the fun of it, they'd have a special green noose prepared with an audience and a clown playing bagpipes to go along with it. Escape. That's what chance I had, so the game started. I let him search and pull himself away from the door, then I would make a run for it, or whichever movement this bloody ankle would alow. I listened deeply for his footsteps as he moved further into the car, blockading himself with junk. I'd have to move soon. He continued to search and once he was on the opposite side of the car, it was my time. I brought myself to my feet, my hands still on the dust-gritted floor, and took the weight on my ankle. The pain was nearly as bad as expected. Excruciating, but there was hardly another choice. I poked my head up to see his back turned. Then I went, hobbling quickly towards the door. I bumped into a crate and his attention turned towards me.

"Hey!"

I leaped off the car, taking the day's brightness harshly in my eyes. There was a thin corridor of grey rocks on side of the track, then green grass, and I came down hard on my bad ankle and fell forward, though I had no time to take in the self-pity of the fall. Kicking up rocks behind me, trying to think of anything but the pain, I stood and ran with an awkward hobble, then turned back briefly to see him lowering himself off the car. Then I sprinted forward, feeling the harsh and unnatural lob in my step.

"I'm armed!" He called behind me. There were woods ahead of me and I ran to them, for there his bullet had a chance of hitting a tree or something other than me. I hoped his gun wasn't yet loaded, and I ran. Energized from fear, I ignored the pain, instead seeing my own death as I waited for that surefire gunshot in my spine, certain it was coming any second.

I reached the wood and continued into the trees. Then I heard a gunshot, but it echoed out, sounding as though he'd aimed the gun upwards. Still, I dove to avoid it. A wind-zip never went by me or a splintering hole in a nearby tree. Only then did I figure he'd aimed up, and that I was safe for the moment, but I had to keep moving. I moved into the wood, further and further. The pain in my ankle came back, starting dull at first. Then the soreness took over rapidly, then into even sharper pain than before. It grew. It felt as though my ankle were clawed in a bear trap. It was a horrible pain, but I assumed, considering my distance on it, that it wasn't broken. I found a tree and hid myself behind it and waited for the train crew to give up and depart again.

About twenty minutes passed before the horn from the locomotive bellowed. Thirst had embraced me like a woman you don't love, my mouth was parched. My back and chest and legs were sweating, and my clothes were wet with sweat. The horn blew a second time, and I began to relax somewhat, sure that the train was moving again, but I wouldn't move until I heard it bellow away into the distance. Finally, it did, and once it was gone, all I could hear were flies and gnats buzzing, and the rustle of nature on the wind. It was cool beneath the shade of the trees, but I was thirsty, and then hunger came over me like a storm that simply appears from nowhere. The path became obvious. I had to go back to the rails and follow the tracks to the next town. The tracks went north towards Jackson. A dangerous path it would be. There were no friends. I was suddenly lonesome, anxious, and terrified.

I remembered the map and tried to dig it out of my bag, but it wasn't there, and after a while, I gave up and tried to picture it from memory. I must have been somewhere slightly north of Lake Pontchartrain. The train ran right between the lakes of Pontchartrain and Maurepas. I thought I should find the shore but was unsure if I was west of it or north of it. I limped north along the track, slowly, my ankle fat and swollen. Often, I had to pause to take the pressure off of it.

An hour passed. I heard the caws from gulls above me, and I saw them like chaotic grey flecks, circling in a wild dance on the air. I followed the cloud of birds in the hopes they were feeding on the water. They were far off though. I walked faster, squinting my face with every step, but the pain was horrible. I couldn't remember a time when I'd been more thirsty, the thought of water titillating my tongue like a naked nymph. Around me, I was surrounded by humid, marshy swampland that was moist and uncomfortable. I was drenched in enough sweat to make my clothes heavier. And I knew this land was filled with dangerous creatures, alligators and snakes and such, but even more dangerous were the people if I were to run into them. People who felt wronged. People under the boot heel of truth, that above them there was something more powerful which threatened their way of life. I in their minds was a faithful servant to this power. The Union. Immigrants. Coming to take it all away. I knew this, and while I was confident I'd get away from a snake, I doubted my chances with an angry man holding a loaded gun.

The pain ran up my ankle to my knee. My entire leg bloody killed and each step sent a harsh jolt upward. Sweat soaked my chest, back, and groin, making me chafe, which made a dandy addition to the discomforts. Ahead of me, I came to a green mound. I changed my course, away from the tracks and towards the old hill, for I imagined there was water on the other side. I hobbled towards it, leading with my parched tongue, longing for just the sight of water. I hobbled on.

I climbed slowly. Each step agonizing. Each step a grueling feat. Yet after reaching the top, the reward was immediate. There she glimmered on the other side, as beautiful as the River Shannon herself. She played sweet music with her gentle waves in the wind, the caws of the seagulls her ambient chorus. Trying to rid my mind of the pain again, I went to her, but hills are unkind to bad ankles. I fell forward, landing first on my face, then turning into a tumble and roll, grunting and collecting bruises on the way down. I smashed onto a flat of small rocks, feeling the sharp pebbles between my ribs and my spine and my ass. I finally came to a stop at the bottom of the hill and laid there for a moment to take in the pain and catch my breath. Stillness came with this moment of hopeless resolve, but then, a voice.

"Are you okay?" Someone asked, a woman's voice, and she spoke in an accent fresh to my ears. When I looked up to see her, shame rushed about me, the type of stinging and potent humiliation that can only be felt when doing something clumsy or stupid in front of a *beautiful* woman. I sat up and looked at her and gave her a wave….like an idiot.

"I'm alright. Just a rotten ankle." I dusted off my clothes and gave my palms a nice blow and morphed my face into a dumb smile. I tied to stand, hobbled and fell once more. She backed away as I fell.

"Are you hurt?"

"I'm alright. Just a bit disoriented."

Her hair was dark black and curled over strong shoulders of dark bronze, her collarbone shaped, her skin darker than having taken a simple touch from the sun, but rather, accepted a long embrace from it. Her eyes were bright blue, like crystals, full of mystery. Of life, it seemed.

"You look like you've had a row with death," she said.

"Yes…A row with death may be putting it lightly. Yeah." I pulled myself up to my feet and tried to hide my limp. She backed away.

"What brings you here?" She asked. "I ain't never seen a man walking along this side of the lake, especially not one in your condition."

"Never planned to be here. Just where the road happened to take me is all."

"Well, that's awfully suspicious, and while you seem like a kind man, I can't have you exploring our land without knowing about who you are. So who are you?"

"My name's Brady, miss."

"Are you from the war?"

"—I am."

"And who do you fight for?"

"Nobody, now."

"What you mean?"

"Listen, miss. You're a complete stranger, so I see nothin' to gain in lying to you. I was a junior lieutenant in the Union Navy, but I've run away from it. Jumped a train to go back to New York City in hopes to be reunited with me mother and sister."

"The Union Navy you say."

"Yes. The Union Navy. But I promise, by God, I mean you no harm."

She paused for a moment, and her eyes were sharp and serious. "It appears, Brady was it?"

"Yes, miss. Brady."

"It appears that someone meant you some harm."

"More than someone ma'am. Likely everyone from here to Virginia."

"Right. And how do you plan to make it to New York like that?"

"Well, believe it or not, I didn't look like this when I woke up this morning. Again, none of this has been apart of any plan. I planned to ride to New York in a train seat."

"Well, you may be stupid, but I believe you."

"Thank you, miss."

"You look terrible."

"You're quite kind. So what brings you to this ghostly side of the lake?"

"My mamma in I live in that cottage, just a half a mile down that way. Just out for a walk."

"You live on this lake?"

"I do."

"Well, it's a beautiful lake. Glad I found it. Can't have taken that fall for nothing."

"How are you going to get on?"

"Oh, I'll be fine. Managed to make it this far. What's the rest of the country?"

"You have a gun?"

I smiled, for it was humorous that I'd made it to such a barren land, miles away from where I was, only to realize that I was not prepared for the road ahead. And silly as it be, the reality had a way of seeping in once under the gaze of, by all I could piece together, a practical stranger with many questions. "No, miss. I don't have a gun."

"Are you trying to die?"

"Again, I see no true gain in lying to you. If I was, it wouldn't be the first time."

"Awfully bad thing for a man on the run to think."

"Right. First and foremost, I'm trying to get back to my family though."

"Have you killed anyone?"

"In battle, yes."

"Outside of battle?"

"—No."

The tension she carried in her body told me how truly afraid she was, though there was some pathway in her questions, as though she were battling some conversation inside of herself.

"No need to be afraid, miss. As I said, I mean you no harm. I don't even mean to ruin your walk. I'll be moving on. Just needed a nice fall to rest my ankle a bit."

"Are you hungry?"

"Not terribly," I lied, calling back to her.

"My momma and I are about to have some supper. You look like you could use a meal."

I was embarrassed enough without the charity, but it was tough to deny that I was truly starving. I didn't remember my last meal. She came closer. Those crystal eyes looked into mine, full of concern. I was hungry.

"It won't be long until its finished. You could maybe have a bath before it is."

If my scent matched my luck, I imagined I was rank.

"I couldn't impose. Really. I'll be alright."

Just the look she gave me, that gentle and expressive squint in her eye saw through a lie as though it were glass. "You're limpin' around like an old grandpa. You're covered head to foot in dirt."

"Are you usually this kind to strangers, miss?"

"Can't say I meet enough of them to know. It's been a long while since we've had any company. You're welcome to supper if you'd like."

A meal sounded wonderful and as difficult as the battle for maintaining my manners was, be they were aimed at lovely woman with a clever attitude, I hardly was in a position to say no. "Alright. Thank you, miss. I'll have to make it quick though. I have plenty of land to cover before the sun goes down tonight."

"You should maybe have a nap first, mister. A prayer wouldn't kill you either."

"A nap and a meal....I'd think you were trying to spoil me."

"From the way you look, some spoilin' from me is hardly going to help. I'm Gabrielle." She reached out a strong hand with this name to shake. So I shook, and she had a strong shake with a soft touch, though her hands were rightly worked. She lead me up the shore and I limped by her side. The lake shimmered in the evening sun behind us.

Fifteen

The cottage was quaint and lovely. The exterior walls once painted white were now a dull, yet somehow charming yellow from wear and weather, the roof unpainted wood, and the structure itself appeared sturdy and well built. She allowed me to freely access the water pump, and I sucked down nearly a gallon. We then went towards the door. After watching me struggle up the first stair of the three leading up to the front porch, she helped me. "Put your arm around my shoulder," she said. The fabric of her dress was soft, and though only a slight touch of my forearm touched her neck, so was her skin. She was deceptively strong and her muscles worked hard to support more of my weight than I wished to give, as I actively tried to force less of it upon her. I'd tightened my hand into a fist to avoid gripping her shoulder as to not make her uncomfortable. She was warm. Her hair and skin smelled sweet, clean, and natural. Once up the steps, I let go of her immediately, sure I smelled. Terrible it is to be conscious of how badl you smell, but I smiled and said, "thanks.", as though I didn't. Her eyes, despite the bit of suspicion they still held, smiled back. She pushed open the wooden door, and it gave a nasty squeak.

"Mamma," she called as she walked inside.

"Gabrielle?" She called back.

"Hi, mamma."

"Where you been, baby? I need help lifting that pot off the stove."

"Mamma. We have a visitor."

I heard the woman's footsteps coming from the kitchen

and my stomach jolted with nerves, shooting through me like thunder. Why, I wondered, was I struck with the feeling of meeting someone important, someone who demanded respect? Then I saw her. The old woman's eyes matched her daughters, bright and crystal blue, however, her's were less pleased to look upon the riff-raff that she saw. The rough expression in her mother's eyes crunched like gravel, and I saw in those eyes how life had eroded her a bit. Taken things away from her and things that she had loved. She held a certain leeriness of trusting in people, and was even less likely to trust a stranger, rightly one limping, covered in dirt, who smelled like a fat kid who'd run a mile.

"Gabrielle. Who is this?"

"My name is Brady, miss."

"Mmm. And what do you want from us, Brady."

"He's come to join us for supper," Gabrielle said. "Surely, you've made enough."

"That's generous of you to offer," she replied, and the tone hinted at a sarcastic nature.

"I don't want to impose or be a burden," I said.

"Oh, hush," said Gabrielle. "We've already had this conversation so sit in that chair and put your ankle up."

"Gabrielle," her mother said. "Can you come help me with something outside." Gabrielle's expression changed to a certain unique reaction which could only exist between her and her mother. She followed her slowly out of the door, and so I sat there alone in the kitchen, a strange and imposing feeling about me, for while Gabrielle was leery of me, and this showed itself in her fear, I got the sense that her mother simply didn't like me upon first sight. Fair enough in my condition, I suppose, bu I felt certain that when they came back inside, my hobble back north would continue immediately, and without supper.

Eventually, the door opened again with a squeak and I turned to see Gabrielle's mother who went straight back to her work at the stove without giving me a glance. Gabrielle followed with two full pails of water. She smiled and said, "The tub is right through there. I brought you some water if you'd like a bath."

I stood to follow her to the washroom. The ankle was in more pain now that I had given it time to rest, the pressure tense, the ankle swollen, fat, and sore. I limped to the washroom where she was already pouring the second pail into the tub.

"You'll probably need another to have any decent kind of bath, but those will have to do. Sorry, it won't be too warm, but we need the stove for supper. I actually prefer cold baths sometimes. They give you a bit of a rush, do you know what I mean?"

Whether or not I did, I had no urge to disagree with her.

"Cold baths are great."

"Good," she said with a smile. "I'll leave you to it then."

"Thanks again."

"You're welcome, Mister Brady." She walked out and closed the door shut behind her.

I secured the latch on the door quietly, then sat down on the floor to strip down. Taking off my boots took a long time. The pain was constant. Then I slipped off my sock and there, the skin was inflated, as round as a fresh pillow, and decorated with splotchy bruises, all part of a large bruise with smaller speckled bruises over. Black and purple was the skin color, and it was right nasty, the smell sour and intense. I tried to stretch the ankle by turning my foot in small circles, but the normal range of motion was less than half. The pain made me hold my breath and bite my lip. Then she knocked on the door. Quickly, I struggled to prop myself up, then hobbled over to the door but didn't open it.

"Yes?"

"Sorry to interrupt. I just wanted to let you know that I've put some fresh clothes just outside the door here. They might be a little large, but they should be comfortable."

"Thank you very much, Miss Gabrielle."

"Supper will be ready soon."

"I can't thank you enough."

"There's no need, Mister Brady."

I awkwardly slid my pants off, maneuvering the sleeve around the sore and bulbous ankle. Then my shirt. I used the old tub for support, lifted up my rotten ankle, and lowered it into the cold water. It brought an odd relief. I slowly lowered myself into the tub. The chilling bite eventually became comfortable, and I relaxed. The weight of what all day had been floated there on top of the chilly water. I cleaned myself slowly, and the small bit of water in the tub changed from clear to a pale grey. I reached over to grab a towel to dry myself. I then slowly finagled my way up out of the tub, went over to unlatch the door, and a cold burst rushed my wet body as I leaned down to pick up the fresh pile of clothes. Outside of the washroom, the house filled with the aroma of cooking onions and garlic, and they smelled delicious. I was starving, so I suppose a stale roll would have smelled delicious. I closed the door again, unfolded the clothes, and they were old but well taken care of. But who did they belong to? I assumed they were perhaps her father's or maybe her brother's if she had one. Whoever's they were, I imagined he was likely fighting in the war. I wondered if his skin color matched that of Gabrielle's, and I imagined that it must. And if he was fighting, what would he think of a deserter standing in his house, wearing his clothes, and eating his food cooked by women he loved.

I went back into the kitchen, uncomfortable in the mystery man's clothes, though I felt fresh from the bath. Gabrielle's mother saw me, still bothered by my presence, and now I felt I understood why.

"Any way I can help?" I asked.

Her mother's eyes met mine for only a moment and I matched the gaze in the hope that she was searching for integrity. I worried that she'd be able to see the foul memories from the war, or worse, the quiet attraction I had for her daughter. I feared that if she could see the tides of war in my eyes, see the loss and the killing, and perhaps she thought that I was one of those sick men who go to war with the joy and hope of killing. Shortly after, noticing the pain in my face as I stood I'm sure, she walked up to the table and pulled out a chair for me, giving it two taps as to say, "sit down." Nothing with her went unearned, I felt. She offered me a glass of iced tea and asked if I'd like a mint leaf in it.

"Sure. That would be nice."

She went out to pick the leaf from the garden leaving me, again, alone in the kitchen. For the first time in days, I felt and was clean and comfortable and sober. No, for the first time in months. Perhaps even the first time since Shane had passed. This thought hit with an overwhelming wave of emotion, remembering Shane though not alone, and I was forced to tell myself I wouldn't wipe dampened cheeks with the sleeve of a flannel that belonged to someone else.

Gabrielle walked back into the room, and I quickly wiped my eyes, though not soon enough before she noticed. Pity me she surely did. She never pretended however to pay little mind, for she smiled, and even came beside me and put a gentle, friendly hand on my back for nothing other than comfort. She must've pitied me. How could a person be so kind for any other purpose? I wondered how lucky I could be, for why of all the lost and pained people in the world did she touch me?

"Hungry, yet?" She asked.

I said yes, with a smile, wiping me cheeks discreetly with the back of my hand. Her mother then came back inside with the mint leaf and went over to the counter to drop it into the tea.

"Young man," her mother said to me. "Would you be able to lift this pot up for me?"

"Mamma, his ankle is in bad shape."

"No, that's alright. I'd be happy to," I insisted, fighting to stand without showing weakness.

She reached out a cloth for me to take, and I went to her, hobbling rapidly as though a fate depended on it, and she gave me the cloth keeping her eyes on the meal, protective of it. She pointed to the large cast iron pot and said, "Don't burn yourself. Just throw it right up there on the table." So I picked it up with the linen in my hand, and it was heavy but I was careful as I limped over to place it on the old table. Her mother came over, then taking the linen right out of my hand to place it on top of the lid of the pot, and as she lifted the lid, the meal billowed in a show of steam. The savory smell of shrimp and garlic rose into the air. She stirred the creamy brown concoction with her wooden spoon and the smell intensified. The shrimp were bright orange, the onions translucent, the peppers and garlic all smothered and stewed together.

"Boy, you stare at the étouffée any harder, you gonna burn your eyes."

"It smells wonderful, miss."

"Mhmm...I know."

"I've never seen anything like it."

"Where are you from, Brady?" Gabrielle asked, having a seat at the table. I took this as a cue to sit, but her mother went back to the stove to retrieve the small pot of rice.

"Ireland, miss."

"How does a man from Ireland end up in South Louisiana?" Her mother asked. "Specially beaten up as bad as you are?"

Their eager eyes both searched me for the answer.

"Long story, I suppose."

"Mhmm..." Her mother smacked a clump of sticky rice onto my plate, then poured three spoonfuls of that perfect concoction over the top before placing the bowl in front of me. The steam from the dish rose, intoxicating my senses. I waited until she had prepared two more plates and sat at the table before I finally began to eat. "Tell us...your long story."

"Well," I said. "My mum, my sister, and I fled Ireland from a nasty potato famine. My father died about a year before we left, but my sister was still young and I was able-bodied, and we were lucky enough to board a ship to New York with the little money we had left. Traveled along with some family friends, one being my best friend." I took a bite of the stew, and the flavor was heavenly, rich with pepper and onions, and juicy shrimp that carried all the flavor of the spices, explosive, and warm.

"Where are your mamma and sister now?" Gabrielle

asked.

"In a part of New York called Hells Kitchen."

"And why are you here?" Asked her mother.

"I was sent to do what able-bodied men are sent to do."

"The war," her mother replied.

"Yes, miss. I didn't have much of a choice I suppose."

"Hmm."

"When I first came to America, I didn't think I would be fighting in the war. I wanted to start a fishing crew. Learn the waters and bays up in New York, find a couple of shipbuilders, and simply work manual labor jobs, or for a fishing crew already existing to raise money to buy my own boat, but the offer for good pay, joining that war effort and all, well, that was hard to pass as you can imagine."

"Plans change," said her mother. "Some people handle it differently."

The room took on an exhausting kind of silence.

"This is delicious, miss."

"I know," her mother said.

We were silent for a while. Then I began asking questions about creole cooking, and her mother answered them plainly as common knowledge with no secrets. I ate three plates, and I believe Gabrielle seemed amused by this. I wanted a fourth but I decided instead to use manners. I finished the rest of my tea, placed my cup on the table, and said, "I should be making my way before it gets too dark." Gabrielle shot me a look, almost as though she were puzzled.

"You plan on traveling tonight?" She asked.

"The sooner I'm back the better."

"Pardon my bluntness, but if you leave in the shape you're in, I don't think you'll make it back."

"He ain't that bad, Gabrielle," her mother said.

"Mamma. He can hardly walk."

"I'll make my way. Always do. Always manage to at least."

"I don't want to insist upon you staying. Just some worrisome instinct I suppose."

"Better to have than not," I said.

"Well, I'd feel awfully guilty to not offer a Navy man a meal, and a night of sleep, especially after the row you've had."

"I'd agree. If I were a Navy man, anymore."

"Who am I to judge your reasons? Just know, it isn't much, but we have a cot. I'd be happy to make it up for you so that you can get some rest before your journey."

"Gabrielle. The man's already said he wants to leave sooner."

"I understand, mamma. But think about walking for miles on some rotten ankle. You know a night of sleep would do it some good."

"You're not wrong," I said, smiling shyly.

"So you'll stay the night then?"

"That's very kind, but you've been generous enough already."

Her mother stood, grabbing her own plate and Gabrielle's and walked them over to the counter. A silent message between them both, no less. "Gabrielle…I'm going to lie down. Be sure you clean up the kitchen before you go to bed."

"Thank you for the food, miss. It may have been the most delicious meal I've ever had."

She looked my direction, her face still stern, unflinching, untrusting. "Glad you enjoyed it." Then she looked to Gabrielle. "Get some rest." The floor of the cottage creaked slightly as she walked across the aged wooded floorboards. The clicking of her bedroom door closing brought about a potent quiet between Gabrielle and me.

"The food was delicious."

"You ate plenty of it for not being hungry."

I smiled. "Care to go see the lake?" I asked.

"Mr. Brady. Why are you so hell-bent on wearing out that ankle."

"I just like to look out at the water after supper. A habit of mine I'd guess you'd say."

"Alright."

She stood and I limped behind her pitifully out into the humid evening. The meal had made me feel better, and while my ankle was in pain, it seemed more manageable. I followed her slowly, up the small hill away from the cottage to the wide lake. There the sun was sinking into the lake like a biscuit into tea, and it cascaded shades of orange and pink and yellow across the clouds above the dark and shimmering water. The water was choppy and with small white caps crashing among the glimmers of the sunset.

There was a log a few feet from the bank and we went to it and sat facing the lake. Someone had put the log there, for I doubted such a perfect seat had fallen there by natural circumstance. We sat before the water, the sky darkening with every passing moment.

"Where were you stationed during the war?"

"Have you heard of the blockade?"

"I haven't."

"Well, I worked on the ships. The Union is trying to block the Mississippi to stop trade between the southern states. War is not good, but I was lucky in a way to see the south. We stopped a couple of places though. Carolina. St. Augustine, Florida, and New Orleans."

"You traveled here from New Orleans then?"

I nodded. "Took a train."

"And you got off here? I didn't think anyone got off here."

"Well...I jumped the train, and then I got caught."

"Why would you do that?"

"Long story, I suppose."

"Seems you're full of long stories."

"I am, I guess."

"And here we are with nothing but time."

So I began to tell her about the Confederate man behind the ticket counter, and she smiled as she listened and I spoke. The sights before me were beautiful, and I was clean and had a full belly. We had a peaceful quiet after the story as I took it all in, the sky behind us growing dark, and the cascading colors before us breaking wild into a slow dance.

"This isn't close to New York. True, I don't know you, and perhaps it's a prideful thing, but I can't help but worry that you have to heal before you take on a journey of that magnitude. And I know the house isn't…extravagant. It's plain, but you can rest here."

"It's a lovely house."

"You'd be in danger if you went out there like this. A cruel world can be hard on a kind man."

"Imagine how cruel it is to the cruel ones."

"Well, the world sure as hell isn't lacking cruelty," she said. "My thought as to why kindness can go a long way."

"You're a pure example, Miss Gabrielle." I tried to move my ankle, proving to myself that I could. Though, I couldn't hide my grimace of pain. "My ankle really is in pretty bad shape."

"Look at it…It looks like it'll be giving birth soon…"

We laughed, staring at it.

"Let it heal," she said.

"Perhaps just tonight then."

"Good," she said, and she smiled, but what did such a smile mean?

It was the first night watching the sun fade behind the ripples of the lake from the bulky knotted seat of that log. It can be surprising, your eyes coming upon beauty so instantaneously, when all seemed so dark and ugly merely hours before. And I thought that the world hadn't changed in the grand scope of everything, but for that one moment, it had. Maybe that's the need for beauty. When the moment's needed, it blinds you from the pain of a dark and horrible world.

Sixteen

We'd watched the sun part beneath the lake, then Gabrielle showed me to their cozy corridor which stored a spare cot. A bedroom it hardly was, but it would do, and it was certainly better than the alternative. I laid on the cot and, fully dressed, fell into the deep, deadened kind of sleep where dreams don't exist and time is infinite.

I woke with my boots still on.

I opened the slender door from the corridor leading outside to see that the morning still disguised itself as night. Aside from my sore ankle, my mind and body were restless, so I limped out to explore the land. I was hungry and felt more so than I had even the night before, but I would wait 'til they were awake. I carried with me impatience, partnered with longing. Longing for Gabrielle to wake. Her kindness in this place had made it feel odd to be alone. That it was less to be so.

Outside, it was cool and less humid than the day before. Blackness and stars were above to the west and from the east bled a faint blueness of light from the coming day. On the ground, I saw shadows of the spidery branches of cypress trees across the land, and a dark mass of shadow trailed behind the night. I limped around to the front of the cottage, trying to loosen the tightness in my ankle a bit when my attention was grabbed by a forest-green, flat-bottomed canoe leaning up against the side of the house. I became excited like a child as a nostalgic feeling of home came to me. Something about seeing a boat in the morning before the sun had risen. It reminded me of my father and our mornings together on the river. It was odd how *these* memories of my father left me with feelings of happiness and longing while most others brought me disgust. And whenever such memories came to me, I often wondered if he carried the same memories with him, and if he did, if he saw the beauty in them. The rather breathtaking simplicity of the sky turning from black to grey while dark water splashed against the side of a boat, or the sound of a casted net slapping against the water for that first time of the day. Though you'd never think it, these things made a profound impact on me. Had he heard or seen the beauty in such things? If there was any man who could have used even just a hint of beauty in his life, it was him. I never thought he liked me much, my father, and it always seemed a mystery when he brought me out on that water with him when I was young. I was useless then, and he certainly didn't like me on dry land. It was as though he were a different man entirely when he was on his boat, still gruff and unsmiling, but content.

I thought I would ask Gabrielle if she'd like to join me on the lake in the canoe. For now, the shore would do. I stuggled limping up the hill, then hobbled back down to see the lake open before me, and above the sky split in lovely blue light across the otherwise darkened sky, the stars of night fading. I lightly stepped over to the rocks by the shore and found a flat one to sit on to watch the new day arrive. The water was still and it hardly made any trickling noise against the rocks. A vast puddle of gentleness. With the quiet of that grey morning, one not so different than the one he was buried, I thought of Shane. I missed him. I missed him dearly. Then a thought came that frightened me. I thought that his death was meant to be. That it was fate. And this was a monstrous thought to have, of course. It wasn't meant to be. It couldn't have been. It could have been avoided. It was a horrible thought.

I wondered what we would talk about if he were by me that very morning on that shore. My mind then moved to her. Gabrielle. I surely would tell him about her. I looked back on the other conversations we'd had about women over the years, and how crude and filthy and awful they sometimes were. Thinking of Gabrielle in such a beastial way, even in the confines of my mind, felt wrong and filthy. Pureness came with thoughts of her, sensual, though not filthy. I imagined her, her brown skin slick with sweat. Her eyes deeply longing for me, so urgently as I did for her. The curve in her lower back, and my palm and fingers running down her smooth skin. My hand running lower still, then taking hold, and the sound in her voice when I did so. Soft sounds from soft lips…but why think of her in a filthy way? Is a man helpless to such thoughts? It seemed unjust that I toyed with the idea of romance after all that had happened. I should have been content and appreciative even just to be alive. I didn't know her. Any reason behind thinking about a woman, especially in such a time must lead to somewhere foul, and she wasn't foul at all. She was furthest from foul. She was gentle and kind and beautiful. All about her made me feel better. And I wondered if she thought of me in this way. I thought that she might, and this brought me goodness inside, and a goodness that I'd lacked for months, or even longer. I wondered if I'd ever felt as good as she made me feel. Of course, I had, I thought, only I couldn't remember a time where such a thought was true.

I was ashamed to think in such a way, for Shane's body was out at sea, down in its depths rotting away with only me to remember him. I cursed myself. I owed it to him and his family to go home and tell them where he was. A heavy pressure hung on my chest that moved outward into my limbs. Upon the grieving thought, my palm pushed to my forehead. Nature had taken him and turned him to nothing.

I heard a squish in the mud behind me, and she was there, holding the hem of her long dress above the mud. Her curls delightfully messy, her eyes slim and tired, and she smiled through stuffy eyes and yawned as she said, "Good morning." The sweetness of it just about stole me away, the same delight of seeing a friend after a long time apart.

"Good morning to you," I said.

"How did you sleep?"

"With my boots on, but well."

"Why didn't you take your boots off."

"Do you never sleep with your boots on? It makes sleepwalking easier. Scuse my early morning jokes. I suppose sleeping was more important than taking them off. How did you sleep?"

"I slept well. Getting acquainted with the lake again? Catching the sunrise?"

"I was up."

"It just kind of falls right into your palms here."

"I'm debating if there's anywhere better in the world to watch it."

"I'm sure somewhere. The world is a big place. Of course, you would know that. You've seen much of it, traveled oceans. You've been to New York."

"I've seen a fair bit, yeah. Have you?"

She smiled. "No. This is the only place I've watched the sunrise."

"Well, it's as good a place as any. The sunrise is not this beautiful in New York. Nothing is this beautiful in New York. This is different, like your own corner of heaven."

"I imagine heaven is vast like the world."

"What part of the world would you like to see?"

"All of it, I think."

"That's a lot of ground to cover."

"I'm guilty that I should want more. I'm a lucky woman already."

"You are."

"I'm free, and don't think, Mr. Brady, that I'm not thankful for that."

"I never thought that."

"It's just that a free woman should be able to go wherever she wants. Any place she wants to see."

"And you will."

"But a free negro can only travel so far...I am thankful though."

"I don't doubt it. And if you want to see the world, you should. I will take you..."

"Oh, Mr. Brady. That's kind, but you know there are many men who don't consider me to have the right. To think that I could see the world." She sighed. "Oh, just thinking about it makes me happy. Does that sound wrong?"

"No…if I may ask, were you born free?"

"I was, yes. My father fled Jackson when he was just younger than I am. He followed the rumors that negroes could find real work in New Orleans, work with a wage, and without an owner. He never told me how he escaped, but if I know my father, I like to think it was dramatic. That may be some rich old bastard died at his hands…Wouldn't that be wonderful? The way he told was that he went down to New Orleans and didn't have much trouble with people trying to turn him in. Said people were different there. But the biggest problem was finding food. So, he goes down to the French Market one morning and steals himself a plum, and he was a big man so naturally, he got himself caught, but the man at the food stand said, 'Don't run.' My papa was thinking he was on his way back to the fields, or jailed, or hanged, but the man instead tells him that if he buys him a beer, he'd let the whole thing go. Papa told him that he didn't have any money and that he didn't know what beer was, so the man asked him, 'You ain't never had a beer?' Then told papa that he had to try a beer, so he took papa to a saloon and bought him a couple, and I suppose that after papa was nice and boozed up, he spilled to the man that he was looking for work. Well, that man just happened to know someone who owned a library and they were looking for some laborer to tend the garden. So papa took the job, and that's where he met my mamma. She worked inside stockin' the books, and she said they used to smile and wave to each other through the window. Then, when he finally got the guts to talk with her, she said she'd teach him how to read. And she did. You see, she was sly. Sees this big handsome man working outside all day, thinkin' he might want himself a good woman, so she offers to teach him how to read. Then she got to pick all the books. All her favorite love stories, and put all kinds of romantic ideas in his head. That's how I came around. By the time that happened, they'd saved up enough money to buy a horse and papa came here and built this place. I grew up here on the lake."

"You must have many memories here?"

"Of course. Almost all of them."

"Which is your fondest?"

"Hmm…" She thought about it. "Being in the canoe with papa. The smell of the water all around. Your hands get so dry."

"Where is he now?"

"He died. Almost five years ago."

"I'm sorry," I said.

I stole a quick look into her eyes, though not quick enough, for there could I see that same grief I'd felt, that perfect unity of our feelings together for such a small sliver of time, though more potent than I'd felt alone. Whoever her father was, I knew in just that short second how much she loved him. How much he meant. And on the account of just meeting her only yesterday without the time to establish a more comfortable familiarity, I decided not to ask her what happened. I simply went quiet, rubbed my chin, and looked into her eyes again, though she now looked away in the distance. My, how her beauty struck me, glancing at her eyes from the outside, and purity carressed you like a vision or a dream. The moment itself, the cool air and damp grass on bare feet, the sun rising, all for her. As though the world itself longed for me to see her.

"That boat…the little canoe leaning up against the side of the house, was that your father's?"

"It was."

"Do you ever take it on the water?"

"Not so much anymore. Why?"

"I didn't know if you ever used it."

"Sadly I don't."

"—Would you like to?"

"Mr. Brady, you're more than welcome. That poor boat has been aching to see the water again."

"Thank you, miss. Truly, but would you go with me? Tomorrow maybe?"

Her eyes took on a more serious look, saddened and stripped down in an instant. She forced a small smile though, regained herself and said, "Sure. I'm sure that would be nice."

"Well, good then." I hid the concern for her change in composure.

"Suppose that means you're deciding to rest up a bit more?"

"Not if I'm going to be a burden."

"Oh hush up, Mr. Brady. It's clear to me by now that you're a good man. Just hitting a rough patch on your road.

"Well, I want you to know how grateful I am for your letting me stay here, and I am willing to earn my keep. I'm not useless."

"I can see that you're not useless, Mr. Brady. You keep good company."

"I can do more than that though."

"You underestimate how nice good company can be."

We went quiet. Water gently crashed upon the rocks.

"So tomorrow."

"Yes. Tomorrow." She said this and the life in her face returned or appeared to at least. So there was something to look forward to. I hardly remembered how simply wonderful and exciting something like that could feel.

Seventeen

I napped for many long hours, folded in a ball on that cot. That afternoon, I woke with soreness all over my body as though I'd been in a drunken brawl just before I had laid down. When I stepped out into the steamy, smothered air, my hair a nest of disarray, she was outside leaning over a patch of soil. Her hands were caked with mud and there were smudges of dirt on her cheeks from wiping away dripping sweat. I just stood quietly and watched her without her noticing me. She focused on the garden with a relaxed concentration in her eyes, content, and comfortable with her work. She seemed in a sense of serene peace, working but carefree. How her gentle expression would change with my calm hand under her chin, imagining her eyes seeking a deep desire within them. A reserved longing. She'd fight the urge to enjoy my touch. How I would feel with her hand on my chest, touching it softly first before pushing strongly against it. How it would feel if her arms wrapped around my back, gripping it tightly, pulling it down towards her body. Feeling the warmth and wetness of the other's early sweat. How she would feel. Her eyes growing wide, bringing on more desire, more meaning, unfolding further, each subtle movement of our bodies meaning more than the last. She, curling her fingers and gripping the skin on my back tightly with her nails, in a place where pain and passion are no different and we seek them both. My hand moving to the curve of her neck, wrapping a bundle of black curls between my fingers and pulling her head back slowly so that she loses herself and must fight to find my eyes again, and she does. Her mouth open. Her eyes closing and opening again with ecstasy. The sounds she makes with each movement, the perfect harmonic notes of raw passion sung through open lips. Two pairs of eyes open to see only each other, both exposing hidden parts of themselves, and in that hidden world behind both sets of eyes lives the feeling that more intense desire must blossom into love. It grows. It grows more powerful, subtle, and real and is the only real thing we've ever known anymore. More real than day to day life. More real than war. Both eyes, mine and hers of crystal, lost and found, surprised, and thankful that someone else so precious could need the other's love. I needed to know if this ever could be true.

A sharp stinger jolted my back and I slapped the spot of the pain. I touched my back and fell the little devil's legs leaving as he took up and flew off into the day.

"Are you alright?" She asked, turning to see that I was there.

"Wasp got me, the little red bastard. I'm alright."

"It's that time of year. Come with me." She grabbed my wrist and led me around the corner of the cottage. There in the ground was a plant with arms like green tentacles stretching itself out. She bent over and ripped off one of the branches.

"Take off your shirt," she said. "Let me see it."

I complied with a nervous curdle in my throat that I tried to swallow down. The vulnerability came in thin wispy clouds. I took it off quickly, button by button, but it felt slow and precise as though I were being watched or judged. My back still stung and through the pain, I tried to avert my mind from thoughts of her, but I wondered if she was having them too. She looked at me, her eyes moving down my chest, then back up into my own. I flexed, slightly.

"Turning around?"

"Right."

"It's just that the sting is on your back…"

"It is."

"Not that I wasn't enjoying the view."

"What's that?"

She chuckled and said, "Nothing. He got you good."

"Who?"

"The wasp. It's swollen up. It's already bigger than my thumb."

"You make it sounds as though you have large thumbs."

"They're not tiny."

"Let me see."

She brought her hand in front of my eyes, and I took it, touching each side of her thumb with two fingers glancing it over. "It's a lovely thumb."

"You're just saying that," she replied, pulling it away.

"No, I mean it. The finest I've seen."

"Hold still." She touched the sting. I masked the grimace of pain with a breath.

"Is that a bit tender?"

"A bit."

Her hand moved down my back. A cool, jelly substance touched the sting and the relief radiated outward. She made small circles on the wound with the tip of the plant.

"Does it feel okay?"

"Yes, but just okay."

She pulled the plant away and rubbed the substance in with her finger before blowing lightly on the wound. Her breath cooled the hot stinging. It was instant relief until she stopped and the heat came back slowly, the pain warming once again, only lighter than before. Then she pulled away.

"That'll do something. It'll be better tomorrow."

"Already better."

"Nonsense. You're trying to hide it by flexing your muscles, but I know it's still burning."

"I'm doing what?"

"Why are men so ashamed of their pain? I don't think I'll ever know."

"You've tended to wounded men before then?"

"Only twice, now."

I slipped my arms back into my sleeves and turned to her while buttoning the shirt. It was always shocking how beautiful she was, how no familiarity ever calmed the sight as though I were seeing her for the first time. It was a vulnerability that felt warm and good. Still, I was nearly in awe as to how beautiful she looked in such simple form as she was, modest clothes and dirty hands and smudges of mud about her cheeks. A woman who carried her weight in the world. A woman who worked and cared and laughed and lived. A woman who gave me hope that there must be a God and that she was the perfected image he'd made her in. A God I hadn't believed in, full of tricks and devises, but a God who had finally given me rest. A God who had allowed me to heal or begin to at the very least. Or was it simply another trick?

Eighteen

Had she forgotten about the venture in the canoe we'd planned? I didn't want to bother her by bringing it up again, but my mind could think of little else. The noon faded into night and I spent it with her, helping in the garden. Much of the time was spent in peaceful silence, which made me wonder if my presence was bothersome or distracting, though occasionally we'd have a short or light conversation which always managed to reassure me temporarily that I wasn't. Her mamma prepared dinner in the house. The aromas of sizzling onions and garlic wafted out hitching rides on the outdoor wind.

I was pulling weeds when I dug my hand deeper in the ground and gripped a thick root. I began to pull while trying to keep the pressure off my ankle, but the root was lodged deep, and forcing it was useless. I put my back into it, but it wouldn't budge, didn't wiggle in the slightest. Then I put my whole body behind it, including the rotten ankle, and the root started to loosen. When I pried it free, it sent me backward, hurling clumps of dirt and mud all over Gabrielle. She blinked with shock. Before she wiped away the dirt, she spat and gave me a dangerous smile before chucking clumps at me. The battle had some good strikes and a couple of hackings, spitting mouthfuls of saturated dirt into the grass. Back and forth we laughted, wiped our faces, and falsely pleaded 'stop', and through dirt-gritted teeth, dry tongues, and filthy clothes, we laughed. We laughed like we weren't strangers. And when all settled again I wanted to tell her then, but I didn't risk the companionship, or perhaps just the plain joyful comfort. What purpose was there in saying what I knew? In a short time, it came, and maybe short it will have lived. I'd let it, this admiration or what it was run the course only hoping that I continued to feel whatever it was that made her voice, her laugh, and her touch feel serene like music that brings gooseflesh to your arms. That despite what pain we might have known, what loss and loneliness, that we didn't have to feel it any longer without the other. I could hope to only feel this joy every day, until my journey back up to the north.

Her mother came outside. We hadn't noticed her, still laughing and covered in mud. She stood behind us, staring, and when we finally did see her, we weren't sure how long she'd been there.

"Are you having dinner again?" she asked me.

I looked from her to Gabrielle, and she smiled. "Yes, miss."

"Well, it's ready." Then slowly she turned and went back inside.

We settled for a moment, clapping dirt off our hands, wiping patches of mud off our faces. Then we went to the well where we took turns, holding out our arms while the other poured water.

We went inside, made plates of rice and chicken at the stove, then sat down at the table. For a while, we were all silent.

"Everything is dying' in that heat, mamma. All that's coming up are bay leaves and a couple of creole tomatoes."

"It ain't no surprise. Happens every year."

"I just don't want us to go hungry."

"We'll get by."

"This is delicious," I said.

"Glad you like it." Her mother said this, then faced her eyes back down towards her plate.

"You haven't been eating much lately, mamma."

"I'm eating just fine, Gabrielle."

"...I like your floral dress," I said to her mamma who refused to look at me. "It's very lovely."

"It was her sister's," Gabrielle said. Her mamma then

darted a look at her as though she'd said something forbidden.

"Oh. You have a sister? So do I…Where does she live? Your sister?"

"She doesn't."

Silence returned to the table in a black cloud.

"Mamma?"

"I'm fine, Gabrielle. Though I would like to know why I am being interrogated."

"You're not being interrogated. We are just trying to make conversation."

"I'm sorry about your sister," I said.

"Yeah. I'm sorry too," her mamma replied.

"I couldn't imagine losing my sister. It would be horrible."

"I don't get the luxury of imagining…"

"Mamma."

"What?" She said, looking up with stern eyes. "What? Do you want to say something? Go ahead." Then she went back to eating. Gabrielle still didn't answer. "Don't do that, Gabrielle. Don't put me in that position."

"I don't understand the problem, mamma."

"The problem is that I do not want to discuss your aunt with a stranger over dinner."

"I apologize," I said, "Truly. It's none of my concern."

"You have no need to apologize, Brady."

Her mother's focus went to Gabrielle before looking away again, her eyes going still, frozen, as if traveling in one or several memories. I knew the look. I'd felt it before. It was the look of finding and revisiting those memories who and what used to feed you. Those elements of those you love which used to make you human, now gone somewhere we don't know. A reality, a source, a spring that left us, replaced by anger or pain as an only recourse.

"I do," I insisted. "It's not my concern. I really do apologize for asking."

"There's no mystery as to what happened," said Gabrielle.

"Gabrielle," her mother said, "enough."

"It happens all the time. It happens every day and there's nothing that can be done to stop it."

"Gabrielle, just close your mouth and eat your food."

"I'm not a child, mamma, and neither is Mr. Brady."

"That's not the matter one bit!"

"Then what's the matter? The only matter I see is that you can't accept what happened to aunt Jeanine."

"Gabrielle! Hush your mouth."

"You can't accept it. Why, I don't know. Tell me, why is it so hard to accept that there are horrible people in this world and that horrible people are going to do horrible things, and fact that they're white just don't matter, not one bit."

"I have! I have accepted the truth and you have not! You are out of line. It don't have a damn thing to do with Jeanine. When's the last time you heard of a negro killing a white man? Tell me, if you're so damn smart. When's the last time Uncle Jim come up those steps after running for miles to tell you that a white man's been whipped so bad that he bled out tied to a tree? And they let him bleed." Her eyes were serious and moistened and full of pain. "How dare you. How dare you disrespect your aunty in this way. And me. Shame on you, sittin' here, showboating yourself around for this white man that come beggin' at our doorstep like a mutt. A white man you don't even know. Shame on you."

She jarred herself from the table, the legs of her chair scraping across the floor. She turned her face away from us to hide us from her tears and left.

Surely, the time to say goodbye would be soon. A day? An hour? Less? There and then I turned to God, that bastard God, and the resentment which had been absent for such a short time rushed back to me, for he had dangled the contentment and joy before my eyes only to pull it away. Damn him for it. Damn him for all the glory men and women gave him around the world. And though I would leave, I felt that I had to tell her about my thoughts. My feelings. I had to make her know, and all of my hope lived in the fantasies of her sweet voice saying, 'I'll come with you.' We would both survive, but only if she came. If she came, I had the strength to face the journey.

I felt how she had been shaken by the talk. Her mother's pain was no business of mine, but I ached to console them both. There in her eyes swam disappointment with herself.

"How are you?" I moved my hand closer to hers though I was nervous to touch it.

"It would be less painful if she could accept what happened. She's been that way for nearly three years. It goes and it comes."

"It's not peace you'll be able to force. It was her sister."

"She's never been that mad before."

"I imagine she hasn't had someone like me sit at her dinner table since it happened. The first time she's eaten with a white man in a while I imagine."

"You're likely the first white man she's had a meal with since the one who owned her."

"Did you know her? Your aunt."

"No. I never met her."

"I couldn't imagine losing my sister. It would be tragic."

"Yes, but tragic enough to deny yourself?"

"Deny yourself what?"

"Your life? Sittin' around, stoopin' all day for someone who isn't there and never can be anymore?"

"It's painful to lose people."

"I know what it means to lose people."

"I don't mean to say you haven't. It's just that I know too. It's a pain that heals like no other I've had."

She looked into my eyes. Her own held some small remorse.

"Who have you lost?"

I hesitated for a moment. Then I told her about Shane. The story had no beginning. I talked about the war and our childhood. I told the stories we would have told together. I told her about the famine, and his family, and his father, and his fiancé. I told her how he died there on the ship in my arms. I deflected every rising motion down within me. For her to truly know how beautiful and pure and good he was, she needed to know him, and if tears fell from my face as I spoke, then a little more faded he became. A little less it was about him, and more it was about me. She deserved to know him. Not the man I became after Shane left. A man who died a little bit himself upon watching him die, only to find that God or the world, or fiancés can be cruel. To show that even the dead can be betrayed. I thought it had killed a part of me until I knew her.

"You're hard on your mother. I know how it feels losing someone you never thought would be gone. It's an ache. A voice in your head that tells you you could have done something to stop it. And that pain you feel, that little voice tells you that you caused it. That you're…I don't know…responsible for it in some way. That it's your fault."

"You think his death was your fault?"

"Not in a way I will ever know maybe…But, without trying. I was leading the battle. I watched him die. There must have been something I could do."

"You're one person. How can one person stop a bullet if they're not the man pulling the trigger?"

"Jump in front of it, I suppose."

"Like that's any better."

"Some men should live before others."

"Stop that. I could hit you for saying something so stupid."

"He was a great man, Gabrielle. He had hope and promise, and a woman who loved him…well, I thought she did. You would have loved him."

"Sure, for your sake. Maybe I would have for you….Why am I saying that? You don't know what I love."

"What do you love?"

She shook her head, almost as though she were annoyed. "I love how we talk together. I love getting to know you, Brady.

And what you're feeling from losing him, that ache…its natural. Why would you feel it otherwise?"

"It's not natural for people to be broken into shambles and left to pick up what's left. To try to find a way to move onto a new life. Because life is different now. One morning, you felt like you knew yourself, then one morning, after he died and I never thought he would…it's like…it's like the past is empty, and that everything you know is good for nothing. The pain destroyed it, the past. It's like you've broken some kind of trust with yourself."

"But you're still you."

"What about the part of me that died with him?"

"Maybe it isn't dead. Maybe it's just badly hurt. Maybe it needs care, and tenderness, and kindness instead of the destruction you keep feeding it."

"I hope you're right, but I don't think you are."

"Be better to yourself."

"I'm better with you."

"What does that mean?"

"…I don't know."

The silence returned. I looked down to see that my hand was still flat on the table and that hers was closer to mine than it had been. Yet, they didn't touch. My hand was burning to touch hers.

"You know what I love?" She said. "Company. Company with kind people. God knows, its a rarity, especially being this far away from everyone. Papa built this far out because he thought it'd be safe, off any chance those old bastards came lookin' for their property. These slavers do that you know. Some of em, they keep searching. And sure as hell, papa was right because you're about the only stranger I've seen wandering around here, and some Union soldier from New York no less. What are the chances we run into a soldier in the south on the right side of the fight."

"It's like it was meant to be…or so it feels. I enjoy talking to you too."

"Tell me about New York," she said this, moving her hand to her lap. "I've only heard and read the stories."

"New York?" I said, confused. "Well, I'd say it doesn't look as nice in the fog. Not like New Orleans. But the buildings stretch down the roads for miles, and it seems that each building is filled with more people than the last. More people every day, coming in on ships, coming up the roads from the south. It's remarkable in that way. Does leave you with a bit of a problem though."

"What's that?"

"There's people everywhere."

She laughed. I loved making her laugh. "I gather you're not fond of that?"

"They're alright. They're abrasive there. Some dislike others enough to fight them in daylight, or even kill 'em if they have the right weapon. But it's not all that different from anywhere else. Everyone eats, and laughs…gets angry. Falls in love. If you're sitting in a pub and a man starts to sing, others will join him while another in the back waits for the right moment to break a bottle over his head."

"It sounds wonderful."

"I don't think there's anywhere as wonderful as where you already are. I imagine I'll have to be heading back there soon though."

"What about your ankle."

"It's healed a great deal already. I'll manage. I think I've maybe overstayed my welcome."

"Oh, no. Mamma will come around. And since you're feeling nice and healed up a bit…I was going to run this by you. I promise I was. I think I'd like to take you up on your offer for help."

"Really?"

"It's just that there are certain chores. Parts of the house that need to be fixed. There's no rush if you could manage, but hurricane season is coming soon and it would be nice to have the roof fixed."

"I'd be….Yes, of course, I'll fix the roof."

"Are you sure?"

"Yes. Absolutely. My God, it's been weeks since I've had any purpose whatsoever."

"That's not true."

"It is, sadly enough," I said, chuckling.

"You're a kind man…and kind men always have a purpose, even if it's just a nice word."

"That's polite."

"Don't think that you're not wanted here. Mamma will be okay. She'll certainly be thankful if you fixed that damn roof."

"I can do that."

"Good…and no rush either. You're still healing." She said this and tapped her hand three times on the table. "I think I'll have a bath." She stood and started.

"Gabrielle."

"Yes?"

"I was hoping to ask you—"

For her hand.

"—if you'd still like to go out on the lake…in the canoe."

She smiled and her hand moved up and took a bundle of her black curls in her fingers. "One day soon."

She turned and went outside to fill some pails of water. I sat down, only waiting for that one day to come. The day where I'd have enough courage to ask her for what I truly wanted.

Nineteen

There had been a storm the summer prior which had partially destroyed the roof of the cottage, tearing away shingles and leaving a steady leak above a bucket inside the corner of the middle room. Each time it rained, you could hear it drip in a steady rhythm, even after the rain had stopped.

There were two challenges. Fixing the roof on my rotten ankle was one. The other was that I knew not how to fix a roof. I'd figure it out. I woke early the next morning after a full day of rain, and limped out towards the woods, for it only made sense that I would need wood. I hiked slowly at first, as I fought the soreness, but the ankle had much more strength than it had a week ago, and so continued outward to the multitude of trees in the distance with the morning sun glaring down, passed the clearing of flat field land, and reached the shade of the front line of cypress trees. I wanted Gabrielle to wake to find me, up on the roof, focused on repair.

The ground beneath the shade was covered in nettles of twigs and mosses and it hid the succulent mud underneath. Squishing my way through, I came across a solid branch protruding from the brown muck, surely good roof wood is what I stupidly told myself. I gave it a pull, feeling the pressure in my ankle, but after forcing it a while, it finally began to loosen as it made fart sounds in the air pockets of the mud.

I sensed the danger only in hearing the sound of the snake's flat belly slithering across the roughage. I froze and scanned the ground. How I saw it, I couldn't tell. It's brown scales camouflaged with the mud. But it came towards me rapidly, and I pulled myself back a steady distance and went still.

It stopped as well. Then it came towards me again and I backed away, attempting to remain quiet. I knocked my heel hard against the root of a tree and fell on my back, and cold muddy water seeped into my pants. But I scrambled up and continued to back away. Then it was gone. The creature seemingly vanished, slithering through the nettles. The solid branch remained far from me. Fear of the loathsome reptile prevented me from going forward any more, worried that he had buried himself beneath the surface. I scanned the ground, searching for movement. All appeared still, so I took another step forward. Then another. A patch of pine needles moved and upon seeing this, I froze, the beat of my heart racing again. The movement was only a light breeze ruffling loose, dry leaves above the surface of the mud. I moved again towards the branch.

I got my hands wrapped around the branch's edge and turned to give the area behind me one more cautious glance before I started forcing it out of the mud again. Slowly, it pried with another plundering fart sound, and I pulled it out and took the weight. It was sturdy and heavy. I lifted it above my head and brought it down to rest on my shoulder, then began to walk back, scanning the ground for snakes.

Out of the corner of my eye, I saw a large log. It was round and wide with a flat surface of bark. I wasn't sure how I would transport it, yet it was too perfect for the job to leave behind. It alone would be enough wood to complete at least half the task. I approached it, puzzled by how it looked, its bark ran in perfect parallel rows down the center, about fifty little ridges that were all about the same size. So perfect that I wondered if that bastard God had blessed me. For the solid bark below, the trunk rounded out, looking almost like a fat belly on an old drunk. I'd never seen a log quite like it.

It hissed, then looking up to the base of it, a black eyeball opened and blinked and I realized that it was no log at all. I thank that same God that I hadn't leaned over to get a grip on and pick it up. Imagine, but a stupid, crippled Irishman lifting an alligator. It hissed again like an angry cat and opened its wide jaws, and I damn near pissed myself. So, I gripped the branch I'd fought hard for and scrambled out of that wood, skipping on my bad ankle, terrified like a young girl.

I returned to the cottage with only the lowly branch collected. I dropped the branch outside, then went in through the side door into the small corridor where I'd slept. There was Gabrielle to my delight, laying down some freshly folded clothes. I yearned to squeeze her for she was the safest, warmest blooded creature I'd seen that morning.

"Where were you?"

"Just hiked out to the woods to gather wood for the roof."

"And you tell no-one?"

"Tell no-one what? That I was going into the woods?"

"Yes, just that. You can't tell anyone that you're going off?"

"I didn't think that….are you upset?"

"I thought you left," she said with pain in her eyes.

"I didn't. Of course, I didn't. I wanted it to be a surprise. I'm sorry. I didn't mean to make you upset."

"It's alright. I'm not upset, I was just worried. Oh, I'm embarrassed for saying anything."

"Don't be embarrassed," I laughed. "Hell, I'm embarrassed. You wouldn't believe how many times I nearly just died out there."

"What?"

"Well, I bumped into a snake, then almost bear-hugged a gator by mistake. I thought he was a log sitting in the mud."

"My, that's exactly what I want to hear. You'll give me a heart attack, Brady."

I was still chuckling, even guilty that I was. "I am sorry. I should have told you."

"It's okay. I just overreact to things."

"I'm sorry."

But she was quiet, and I felt clear that she wasn't yet at ease. But why had she worried? Was it stupid to believe what I so wanted to be true? There at that very moment, was the first time we'd stilled and quieted each other, each with nothing else to say. Still, I was content with just her presence. Just her being there. There was just her. The only person to care about where I was. And was it now that I didn't want to be anywhere else, but with her? What about my family?

I told her I would get started and she went in to do some chores as I spent the afternoon sawing wood. The noon trickled into the evening, and she came outside barefoot, her black curls tied behind her ears. There was a freshness about her. A feeling that she'd grown acquainted with the morning's awkwardness and found a way to grow from it. She smiled at me then gestured for me to follow. She brought me to the side of the house where the canoe was flipped.

"Still want to go out, then?" She asked.

I hid my subtle smile which internally was more of a beam. Together we picked it up and started towards the lake.

My boots squished in a mud puddle. Once we got the boat into the water I sat down and took them off before climbing into the boat. I stood up, refreshed by the boat's grit on my heels. I reached a hand out to her and she took it as I guided her onto the boat which wobbled slightly. We both sat and I began to paddle out. The tip of the paddle splashed and disappeared into the brown murkiness of the brackish water. We were quiet. We heard only the ripples of the small caps on the waves breaking upon each other. When the sky began to change color, all was muted and peaceful and I looked from the sky to the water, to her. I stopped paddling and let us drift.

"It's beautiful." As she said this, I saw a change within her. She broke into a vague smile for only a moment before traveling deep into the depths of her mind, and it was clear in her eyes that a deep sadness lived. "It makes you believe that you belong where you are. That there's a reason for belonging," she said.

"A reason?"

"Yes. A true reason. Even if you can't see it."

"You mean that God has a plan?"

"Maybe. Maybe something more important, as though God himself created something that even transcended him. Something that makes you feel safe, despite all the pain life has in God's plan. I suppose that's what I'm saying."

Then a harsh memory came to me. We went still, stayed silent, and continued to look at the sun setting over the choppy water of the lake. I thought of him. Thought that since she'd told me about her dead father, that I should tell of mine.

"I never liked my father much," I said. "Have I told you that?"

"You may have mentioned it. Why?"

"I never did. I loved him, perhaps out of obligation when I was young...but his character was repulsive. He was a devastating drunk. Favored hard beatings, and he hit hard too. I hated him in ways. Then he'd take me out on the water. That's the odd part, you see, was that on a boat, I didn't want to be with anyone else. He was something like a hero on the water. A strong man who could do no wrong. He made you feel safe, but only on a boat."

"Why do you think that was?"

"I don't know. He wasn't much of a talker. Very quiet. Reserved when he wasn't drunk, that is. There was one morning though when he took me out on the river, and we stayed on that river from the moment the sun rose until it set that very same night. And at the end of the day, as we were heading back to the docks, he asked me... 'how do you feel?' It was an odd question, from him, odd for him to care about how anybody felt, and I was so shocked by the question that I lied. I lied and gave him the answer he expected. I just said I was good and tired. But the truth was that I was happy. I felt like I belonged there at that moment. It may have been the happiest I've ever been with my father... Does that sound stupid?"

"It's not stupid."

"Well, perhaps it was pointless then. I'm trying to say that lying to him, on that day, in particular, is something I regret, small as it sounds. Right after, he looked at me and he said that there was a power on this river that I'll grow to respect. He said it's a force you can feel with your fingertips. You can hear it in the sounds of the waves. You can smell it. And he said that the force comes from the souls of the men who have dedicated their lives to the water. The sailors, fishermen, and captains. They lived on the water and died on it just the same and the only people who can feel that force are the people who are destined to do the same, son. People like me. And when you finally feel it for the first time, part of you will rest with the water. It'll calm you. He said that I'd feel it myself one day, and I did. The water is never the same after you feel that for the first time."

"Do you believe it."

"I have to. I used to believe that the only reason my father told me that was so that I didn't forget him when he died. But since Shane died, the water has been the only thing to settle me when I'm lost. I feel what he meant. It makes me angry sometimes that I do…and depresses me, and it doesn't make me love him anymore, but I can't stop thinking about the idea. I suppose it's not a terrible idea if it's true. Better than giving him what he wanted. The water doesn't make me remember him."

"It does though," she said.

"No. Shane is the one I remember. Shane is the one who deserves to be remembered."

"Maybe that feeling isn't insane or mystical. Maybe that feeling is simply love."

"Right. Well, that would assume that my father loved me."

"Perhaps he did. Perhaps, even against what you say, you love him. Is it so hard to believe?"

"Yes, it is," I said, suddenly serious. "Nasty brute of a drunk didn't love anyone. Broke me arm once, he beat me so hard."

"I didn't say he was a good person, but just because someone isn't good doesn't mean that he couldn't love or that he didn't need to love."

"He didn't deserve love."

"Of course he did."

"No, he didn't."

"Is this about you or him?"

"Me?"

"Yes, you? Why?"

"Why what?" I sneered. My guts felt like kindling blown aflame.

"Why don't you think you're deserving of it?"

"Of what?"

"Of love."

"Who said that?"

"Is it because of your father? You believe he never loved you."

"My father didn't love me. My father didn't love anything but his fuckin' bottle."

"For the life of me, I'll never understand. Why are people? Why are you so troubled by death."

"Who's talking about death?"

"It's clear you've never accepted or came to any kind of reasoning with your father's death...and you're mourning. You're grieved by it."

"I'm grieved by Shane's death, and that's because he was my friend, a brother, and that doesn't mean that I'm troubled by death."

"You know that Shane loved you. You're troubled by your father, and you're denying the possibility that he ever loved you, and that's why you suffer. This isn't about Shane. It's about you, and your father."

"What do you know?"

"I do, Brady."

"Take it back."

"No."

"Gabrielle."

"I will not, Brady."

"You have no right to say it."

"I have every right to say whatever I like."

"You don't. Not with this."

"Says you."

"Yes, says me."

She smiled in an attempt to make the conversation playful, and I could have hit her. Never had a smile made me so angry.

"Is this some cute topic of conversation for you?"

"Of course not. But it's a conversation. A crucial one."

"You don't know what you're talking about, because you don't know me. What do you know, anyway? What pain do you know? You don't know anything. You haven't sat there and watched your friend's life... his life fade away in your arms. Gone in an instant after a lifetime. You haven't been on the deck of a ship, standing through a wake that never ends, watching man after man talk about what other dead men meant to them. You haven't lost your father and felt nothing! Absolutely nothing, and then be expected to be able to live with yourself. At least when you lose a best friend and feel pain, you know that you're not the heartless garbage your father was. But what would you know about any of that? You wouldn't. You don't. You've never seen anything more than this fucken' lake."

There was a pause. "Finished?" She asked.

"Excuse me?"

"I said are you finished. Trying to stab me, man."

"That's not what I was..."

"My father is dead too. I told you that. He's buried in this lake. And you don't see my mother crying about him at the dinner table, do you? He wasn't a nice person, Brady. But he was still loved, and is deserving of it."

"If only it was that simple," I sighed, catching myself battling that urge to fight like a nosy drunk. But there in her eyes, oh how I saw the conflict eating away at her. She, alone with a brute who'd pulled her away from the shore. The sight of her in pain, especially that caused by me and my anger, ate at my soul. "I'm... God, Gabrielle. I'm sorry. I didn't know your father was buried here. Not here on the lake."

"No, you didn't know. Yet, you try to tear me to shreds because you can't make peace with anything. Not your friend, not your father, not…What do you think you're going to gain by tearing yourself apart?"

"I don't know…"

"You don't know. Do you ever think you should know before you start telling someone that they're incapable of feeling anything that you feel and swinging at people who you don't know? Who you just mark off as something less because they've lived in the same place their whole life."

"That's not what I was trying to do."

"What were you trying to do then? Because that's exactly what you did."

There was quiet again. The waves.

"I'd like to go back," she said. There was nausea in my stomach. I handled the paddle and pictured us from afar, a small canoe where inside sat a beautiful woman and a brute. But the brute only wanted her. But brutes do what brutes do, smashing everything in sight, even what they love.

When we reached the shore, she said nothing. She simply stepped out of the canoe and walked out towards the house. I watched her until the closing door blocked my view of her, and once she was no longer there, the quiet brought with it the recourse of what I had done. Despise me, I did. And with a head so full of nasty and regretful thoughts, I paddled out into the lake again, the orange sky slowly fading to black. She was in my thoughts, but I was alone.

Over the water again, I stared down and thought. Then I dug in my pocket and pulled out Shane's whistle. Perhaps it was the night that I would play it.

Twenty

Funny that earlier in the afternoon, I thought only of how I would ask Gabrielle's mother for her blessing. Funny thing that would've been. Even if the blessing were granted, how would Gabrielle say 'yes?' There stood ole' Brady Gallagher in the canoe, the wood between me and the peaceful lake, with anything but peace about me, craving a drink once again. For just one giant swig of whiskey. Here, his father remade over. A coward that was undeserving of love from someone so beautiful and pure as her. I'd likely have been a mad, miserable husband.

Between the mild and rocking waves, I heard the sound of a whistle, but not a screech I had blown myself. It was sweet and well-played. I looked upward, trying to see where it came from, and my heart jumped into rapid-fire. Then the sound came again, this time softer and behind me. It was damn near mute it was so soft, but I listened closely for it. It was music. A song even. A song that Shane used to play those nights we perched on the deck of the ship.

"Hello? Who's there?"

The song stopped and the sounds of the waters rose again.

"Who are you?" My pulse pounded in my wrist. I looked around full of suspicion but heard only the waves once more. "I'm warning you!"

The music returned. It came in a light echo on the surface of the water moving closer to me and for me, I was certain. I felt my anger and suspicion lowering down like a tide, revealing my pain caked beneath like barnacles. The music let it show, the wound. The hatred for my father. The self-loathing parts of myself that I'd adopted from him. My guilt. Shane leaning on the rails of the deck, playing that lusterless whistle as each sweet note stripped me of a little more of myself, a piece of me I'd created to hide the pain. Then the part of me I denied. The loving side of me. Gone the old Brady almost was. Drowned in his horrible pain. Drowned in the victimization of what he couldn't control.

Perhaps this was the feeling my father had spoken of. The feeling of men who belonged to the water. The feeling that made you sure you'd end up there. I felt it there on Lake Pontchartrain. A painful negation with myself, and acceptance of responsibility or purpose that I had refused to feel until this moment because I had hurt the person I loved the most. She saw right through the paper cut out of myself that I'd created and flaunted, that painful soggy victim who then resembled the whole of who I was. I knew that I'd not been myself and that was all.

I knew that I missed Shane. I knew that I loved her. I knew that I never knew my father, and that knowing him no longer needed to matter. I knew that I was a coward and that I couldn't be any longer. I stared up at the florescent moon, brightly beaming glimmers onto the water of the lake, and I knew what I needed to do.

Twenty-one

Though I hadn't slept much, I woke early the next morning and began sawing panels to fix the roof. After only two hours, I had a sore arm and thirty wooden panels. I went into the kitchen to make some coffee and Gabrielle was scrambling eggs. She asked me if I'd like some with little vivacity. After waiting for the coffee to finish, I poured myself a cup, and she held a plate of eggs out to me. I smiled and said thank you.

I joined her at the table and we ate and sipped coffee in silence. Uncomfortable slurping and clinking forks sounded though a silent tension, like a growing typhoon heading for shore. Unable to hold the silence anymore, I finally spoke.

"The roof should be done by tomorrow. Should only take one more trip out to the woods."

"That's great. Mamma and I are appreciative."

"Where is your mamma."

"Out working with the chickens."

"Just curious." And the silence returned. "Gabrielle. I owe you an apology for last night."

"You don't. You made your point clear and truthful and that's all that matters."

"I didn't though. I was taking my shit out on you because for some reason I don't know, I blame myself…for both of them. And you…you've been so good to me. You took me in when you didn't have to and you're the last person I want to turn away just because I can't take responsibility for my…I'm sorry's all."

"You don't have to say this, Brady."

"What?"

"These problems are your own. Please don't bring them

to the table."

"...Okay."

I clinked my fork on the plate, scooping a bite of eggs. I went to bring them to my lips, but I stopped and put the fork down.

"Gabrielle...I love you."

Her fork dropped to her plate. She looked up at me. Those haunting eyes, full of disbelief and a certain beauty. I'd never seen them give such a look.

"What?"

"I love you. I have no doubts. I love you to fucken' pieces."

"Is that..."

"That's what part of last night was about, surely. There are things I'm figuring out with Shane and my father, but I've known about you since the first day when you found me rolling down that hill. I looked up and I knew it. I loved you."

"This is..." She paused, trying to straighten out her thoughts. "I think, I think I love you too, Brady. I mean that. I do."

"That's wonderful," I said, and felt a smile crease my face.

"I have to go lie down," she said and stood. "I don't feel very well."

"...Okay."

And oddly, she pushed her chair away from the table with her thighs, stood, and walked to her bedroom. She closed the door behind her and I didn't see her for hours.

Twenty-two

A full day later, after only one more trek through the woods, I hammered the final panel into place, gripping the shingle tightly and pulling it to see if it would give. Strong enough to hold up through even another storm. I climbed down. Looking up at the house from the ground right there gave me pride in the cottage. I caught myself wondering about what other small projects may have needed repair. Distantly, since telling Gabrielle how I felt, these projects felt like my responsibility. I wanted to give her the space she needed, but I had hardly seen her for the past two days. How did she feel? Did she want anything from me? Did she need anything? Was our love an fate and a potentinal yet to be discovered?

I poked my head in the cottage and shouted that I was going for a walk. I headed out towards the shore, letting my mind fill and flow. Shane had died to lead me here. Shane had to meet Sarah-Beth so that I would have a reason to find her. And after she hurt me with the news of her engagement, it gave me a reason to abandon the war and head north. It gave me a reason to jump a train and get caught and hurt my ankle so that I could hobble to the very doorstep I was now walking away from.

I went back to the shore and waited, calling silently to Shane through the whistle on the waves. "I've found her," I said. I played the whistle, perhaps poorly but with a full heart. "I found the one who I'd spend the rest of my life with, and how you would love her too. She would love you and you would love her if you ever could have met. Shane, you would be so happy now, here in this free and open land. We should have run away from the war from the start. We should have. We would have saved you. It would have been a difficult road even if we would have left, but we should have. It was what we wanted. We didn't believe what we were fighting in. But would I have met her then? Was this all a purpose Shane? How could I ever say that your death was for some purpose greater than even who you were?"

Suddenly I heard her slow, barefooted walk towards the water where I stood. How beautiful she was, a face so dark and whole, with stunning eyes full of mystery. And when she came, I felt whole, for I'd been waiting for her. How it filled my heart with joy. The sight of her eyes and the black curls that fell over her shoulders. How full and human she made me feel. How one with life, even that which was grim and dark and horrible had paved a meaningful path that eventually led me to her. That even the most forlorn, gone cases of men and women could find their way to each other. I had. She had brought me out of the darkness of hell, the hell of my mind, and how I owed her for it. I owed her my love, my life.

"Hello, Brady."

"Hello," I said. "My God, if you only knew how happy just seeing you makes me feel."

"That's very kind."

"Kindess is hardly my purpose...The roof is finished."

"That's good news."

"Gabrielle, where in the world would you like to live?"

"Paris?" She said, joking.

"Well, you and I will go to Paris."

"Brady..."

"We will. And we'll live there as long as we're happy. Then we will pack and move to the next town and the next until you and I have seen the world. By that time, we'll be old and angry and full of life."

"That's a fine thought."

"Let's go. We'll go to Paris."

"My mother used to read me the Count of Monte Cristo."

"We'll go there too. Monte Cristo, wherever that is."

"Brady..."

"Gabrielle. I can't stand in the shadows and pretend anymore that all we have right now is enough. It isn't. You've done everything possible for me and I have so much to give back to you, and I want to give you my life. A life of adventure and a life that you've never seen beyond this shore."

"I have a life."

"I know. But I want to make it better as you have for me. I want to bring you that same joy, even if it's just an inkling of that joy because what you've given me can't even compare."

"Brady."

"I can't believe with all the truth that I know that I would be alive today if I never would have met you. You and one kind old man are the only people that have separated me from death, and I can't imagine that if I were to go on, that I could do it without you."

"Where is this coming from?"

"Because you have to know all of what you mean to me. I owe you the world."

"You don't owe me anything. I've told you that from day one."

"Oh, but I do. Because I'm a different man now, Gabrielle. I'm a man with a purpose, and my purpose is you. It's to give you everything that you could ever want out of life. It's to be a lover to you, and a friend, and every other role that a man can play while he still breathes."

"Please don't..."

"Don't what? Gabrielle, I must. I have to. That's why we met. Because God, a God that I didn't well believe in a month ago brought us together. And we'll go on. We'll go on through this horrible, bitch of life together by each other's side, and we'll make the best life out of it. I love you, Gabrielle, and I don't want to go on another day of this life without you by my side... Will you marry me?"

"Brady," she said. And her eyes swelled with tears. "That can never be."

"Gabrielle? Please. Think about what we can have together."

"I can't think about it, Brady. I'm certain that it could never be."

"Because of your mother?"

"No. Because I love another."

"You?"

"Yes, I do."

"But where? Where is he? Why isn't he fixing the roof?"

"He is in the Navy. At sea fighting for the Union. He left to join up after New Orleans was taken. A runaway slave, just like my father. But when the war came, he wanted to fight. I have not seen or spoken to him in nearly a year."

I had to turn away, collect the truth of where my life was going. "You never thought to tell me?"

"I never saw a reason to. I never saw a reason you should know."

"You never thought that I could fall in love with you?"

"I never thought you would."

"And you never thought that you could fall for me too?"

"I can't, Brady. I'm true to him."

"You did though. I felt that you did."

"I didn't, Brady. I'm sorry, but that's simply not true."

"But you said you loved me."

"I do, but it can't be romantic. It simply can't be. I'm sorry. I really am."

"...Yes, I'm sorry too." I hid behind hard and sullen eyes.

"It's nothing to be ashamed of."

I laughed involuntarily. Tears nearly bombarded me again, but I stopped myself, unable to gauge how I truly felt in the moment "I feel like an idiot," I laughed. "Excuse me." I began to walk away. Oh, how frustrating it is that the mind doesn't grasp the situation until after it has happened. Embarassment coated me. Then anger. The type of anger Sarah-Beth had filled me with as she spoke. Betrayal, lighting like a fire beneath my gut.

"Of course, your roof is fixed so there's no real reason to

keep me around anymore," I said this with my back turned.

"Pardon?"

"The chores are done, so let's just send the help on his way. The weary traveler can leave because we've already milked him of his labor."

"Brady. I know you're upset, but you're a better man than this."

"I'm a better man. A depressing war-torn fool. What a good man. Can't get over his friend, hates his father, and can't love the only woman he loves because he's a good man. But there's a better one out there, somewhere lost at sea. What a joy I am."

"Don't speak ill of him. Do not. You don't know him."

"Fine. Must be a fine man."

"He is a fine man."

"Even though it's quite likely he might be dead."

I watched as she blinked tears onto her cheeks, clear that the thought had crossed her mind well before that moment. The sight of her tears shed for him only enraged me more.

"Have you ever thought about what war is? The hateful, useless bloodshed that happens on those waters. Death is more rampant than a common cold on one of those ships."

"You're cruel," she said. I felt justified in my anger and I justified to myself that she was deserving of such torture. For life had given me nothing but torture. Toyed with my heart, attempting to feed it happiness, just before God, the bastard, ripped it away beneath a twisted ankle. But her head was down. She looked up at me with glistening eyes. Shock piercing through those beautiful crystal eyes. A look that she was seeing a man who she didn't know existed before that moment. A look that punctured me with sadness. A monster, I was. I'd done it again. Crushed what I loved with uncontrolled anger. Oh, and the pain of that guilt is so particularly crushing to live through, for the worst part is that only you are responsible. You are to blame. Nothing prevented you from being the good you know you can be but you.

"Oh, God. Don't cry. My God, I'm sorry. I'm sorry I said that."

She shook her head. There was nothing more to say. She wiped her eyes while shaking her head and she walked away, back towards the cottage.

"Gabrielle..." I called, but she didn't reply, and with a back turned, I could hear her muffled sobs as she walked away. And there I stood alone on the banks of that peaceful lake, wondering to myself if the old man ever should have saved me.

Twenty-three

I sat on the banks of the lake for well over an hour. The sun began to set, closing on the final night I would spend there. The guilt within me was immense. Many thoughts had infiltrated my mind of my hypocrisy. How could I treat her that way if I loved her? How could I love her less for remaining true to the love she called her own? She was every bit a great woman. She was the great woman that Sarah-Beth never was. And here I was, a brute and a monster, torturing and destroying a pure woman who had done exactly what Sarah-Beth hadn't. Who had been the kind of woman that Shane, or any decent, honorable man deserved.

It was time to leave. It was time to tell this wonderful place goodbye. This place gave me revival and fair memories that were needed to continue on. This place that had healed me just before I destroyed myself again. Though stunted, looking out onto the water, I remained still, unable to rid myself from the thought that there was more to be done. That perhaps the foundation could be repaired instead of leaving it in a dust pile behind my shoe prints. She likely wouldn't even speak to me.

On a whim, I slid Shane's whistle out of my pocket. I brought it to my mouth and gave it a gentle blow. The sound that came out was soft but off, so I adjusted my fingers and blew again. The sound still sounded wrong, so I continued to blow, gentler now, adjusting my fingers until the sound I wanted rang out in a perfect pitch. Then this continued as I tried to recollect the notes that I liked, experimenting with new ones until a combination of them formed into some semblance of a tune. Night came over the lake and I continued to play. I never quite got it right, but I kept playing, casting that soft tune over the water and it echoed on the waves before me. My mind was wiped of any torture. There was only the sounds of the music and the water, only the problem of solving the note before the next, and the struggle of timing each. Eventually, the whole song played out peacefully and sad.

I woke with the warmth of the sun shining down on me, the whistle still in my palm. I sat up and looked and thought I'd give it another try. My progress from the previous night had improved, and to my surprise, I played a song that was the foundation of something lovely.

I had to talk to her. A true apology was needed. I didn't expect her forgiveness, but continuing on without an effort assured me that I wouldn't make it back to New York as someone whole. The man that separated me from my father. I knew I had to revive him and that began with Gabrielle. Drenched in sweat, I slipped the whistle back in my pocket and stood and started towards the cottage, a stranger all over again.

I knocked on the door and waited. Then it opened and she stood there in the doorway with a perplexed look in her eyes.

"I thought you left?"

"I couldn't. Not without saying goodbye."

Her face creased with sadness. She brought her hand up over her eyes.

"Gabrielle, I never meant to hurt you. I did, but I didn't intend to."

Each silenced sob coming from her lips set my heart aflame. Each bit of pain I felt throughout. "You're not a bad man," she said.

"I may be, but I never wish to be when I'm around you…"

She settled in, listening. "Why don't you come in. Have some breakfast before you go."

I nodded and went in. The clothes I had arrived in were

now clean and folded on the small cot in the back corridor there. I changed into them. They smelled like soap and faintly like her. I shouldered my bag and went into the kitchen where Gabrielle was making eggs, and while she cooked, I sat at the table.

"This will be greatly missed," I said. "The company. You should know that."

"I remember being young when my papa would return after a couple of days in New Orleans. He'd poke his head in the kitchen trying to get a whiff of whatever was cookin'."

"Do you find that you're like him?"

"My pappa?"

"Yes."

"Same personality. Very emotional. Yes, I'm very much like my father. A spitting image"

"You say that with so much pride."

"I loved him."

"I can see it."

"You're not your father, Brady. No more your father than I am. The man you spoke of doesn't sound like you."

"And what about yesterday?"

"What about it? It's not that I don't love you, Brady. It's only that I promised myself to someone, and if I don't keep that promise, what value does it hold, regardless of who I make it to. I can love who you are…there's no moral crime in such a thing. Of course, I love who you are, but we are not meant to be. It's only that simple."

I sighed. "…I suppose you're right."

She walked over and placed a bowl of grits and scrambled eggs before me.

"I'll never forget our time," I said. "I'll remember you, and that's a promise."

At this, she smiled. She sat and we ate. I got up and poured us two tin cups of coffee.

"You know, shortly before Shane died, he had fallen in love," I told her. "He fell in love with a beautiful woman, a wealthy one in New Orleans. Asked for her hand, and she granted it. His dying wish was for me to find her and tell her what had happened. So I went back."

"And what did the poor girl say?"

"She was engaged. It made me feel awful, as though I was the one who was betrayed… It was because I felt pity for him, and pity was never something I'd felt for him before, not ever. Not once when he was alive. I was never supposed to feel that for him."

"Why do you say that?"

"Because he was just a better man. He was someone who would have kept a promise until his dying day."

"Alright."

"I hope that your man is alive and finding his way back to you, I really do."

She gave a smile which changed quickly to a frown of longing. "You're a good man, Brady. A kind man."

"Thank you for all that you've given me."

I stacked the plates and brought them over to the counter. Then I shouldered my bag and walked towards the front door of the cottage. She followed me. I turned to her and gave her fine eyes one more deep glance, hoping she felt my appreciation. My love for her.

"Goodbye, Gabrielle."

"Goodbye, Brady."

We hugged each other, tightly and true. Then I turned and began to walk north. I gave her a final wave, then walked away from the cottage. Away from her.

I walked with a light limp along the shore of the lake for many miles. The cottage was out of sight. Although I was thirsty and my ankle was sore, there was a revival within me. Something new and bright which radiated within my very veins. Call it hope, perhaps, or courage, but whatever it may be, it had new strength to continue on.

I stopped to take a short break, sat on the grassy ground, and enjoyed the sight of sunlight reflecting and dancing on the surface of the water. I took a breath of the semi-salty air, wiped my forehead of the sweat that accompanied the heat. And I thought about God and angels. Thought about Gabrielle. Thought about Shane. Of life and of loss. But how a journey must continue. I bumped the small lump in my shirt pocket, Shane's whistle it was, and I reached in and pulled it out. Thought deeply of his eyes and how they would cast upward to the heavens whenever he heard some music. And I hoped deeply that whereever he resided, the notes flowed in plenty. That the sounds cascaded off the surface of the water in whatever peaceful body he'd found. He found his peace in the music, I knew. I knew that Shane had his love all along. A love which simply couldn't betray, for it harmonized with the rhythm of his life. I sat basking in the warm sunlight and played to waves on the water. I played the sweet song I'd written for Shane to finally hear, certain he heard it somewhere if God or love be true. And when I reached New York, I would raise a glass to him, and sing a song of a beautiful creole girl on the banks of Pontchartrain. I'd sing the song for Shane to hear, the beauty of the lyrics incomparable to her own. He'd know I loved them both.

Acknowledgements

One of the biggest joys of creating is thanking the people who helped, but a simple thanks is an understatement to the people I'm about to acknowledge, many of whom without, this novel wouldn't exist.

I'd like to start by thanking, John McKnight, the editor of *A Whistle on the Waves*, who from the beginning made clear to me his genuine love and appreciation for fiction, which in this technological day and age, is about the most encouraging thing a young author can hear. John managed the impossible, walking a tight rope of sternness and warm-inducement, and never shied away from the ultimate goal of keeping the characters true to themselves. He holds a gift in his criticisms, which somehow affirm one, rather than tear down. He has a wonderful ability to walk into the dark and sometimes lonely world of your story, and acknowledge the characters' lives for what they are, lives. True grace and goodness live in the work John does, and he should be acknowledged and thanked for it. So thank you so much for your effort and care with this work that was so dear to me.

I want to thank Jake Kinney, Eddis Brown, and Dean who were kind enough to house me on their couch in Brooklyn during the early drafting days of this project. Those few months were some of the richest of my life.

I want to thank Jared Kelly who spent many nights with me in Manhattan bar rooms, letting me vent about these characters over several beers and shots of Jameson. Thank you for the friendship you give which goes far beyond any work we'll ever do.

Thank you Peter Smith who's never been short of an encouraging word, or a great conversation. I believe in you as much as you believe in me.

Thank you to Donna Foster who is a great teacher and impacter of lives.

Thank you to Idella Johnson for the beautiful work you performed in the promo. You captured Gabrielle's beauty with subtly and grace.

Thank you to the editors and musicians of the promo, Nick Gagnard and Dylan Young, both for your advice, effort, and kick-ass work on set and in the editing room. You guys were fuckin' rock stars who managed to pull the sound of a tin whistle literally out of thin air. Thank you for your ongoing friendship through the years since high school, and here's to many more.

Thank you to Christopher Ramage who fills the best roles a friend can fill. You're never shy of a joke, a soulful two-hour phone conversation, a glass of scotch, a cigarette or seven, a word of advice, a good fuckin' time, or the occasional room when passing through Atlanta. You helped push this book forward in more ways than you know, and your work on the promo was so good that it breaks my heart. Love you, dude.

Thank you Coach Donald Hood for the constant love and support. Since the day our paths were fortunate enough to cross, you've become one of my favorite people to talk to and share a meal with. You've brought nothing but joy into my life and will forever remain a mentor as well as a dear friend.

To Mrs. Elma Sue Hood, there aren't enough words to write. Not only did you help to make this beautiful book cover, but you've given so much more to me and to the world. The joy of getting to know you and your family through the years has helped me discover the better sides of myself which used to be clouded in bitterness. Simply being around you and your family give me the belief that true happiness is attainable. Thank you.

Levi Hood. I know for certain that without you, this book would not exist. You directly impact the narrative and you directly impact me. The design you created on the book cover turned out better than I could have imagined, and you already know it, but more importantly, you're my harshest critic and my best friend. There are memories with you that I wouldn't trade for the greatest riches in the world. There are conflicts with you that have humbled me into a better person. You're the only person I know of who I shoot the bird at one minute, and tell a joke to the next, and I don't even like to think about who I'd be without you in my life, for it would be so stale, dry, and boring that it'd resemble and three-week-old baguette. I don't hope, but expect, that we will remain life long friends until one of us kicks the bucket, as states the definition. Perhaps one day we'll wack each other with our canes, then have a cry like a bunch of bitches. I love you, man.

To Dad, Collin, Chandler, Paw Paw Bob, Maw Maw Carol, and Maw. Your love and support mean the world to me. You challenge me every day to be the absolute best I can be, and whether you know it or not, none of these creative endeavors would have any life without you. Thank you for your constant love.

Mom, you encourage me every day without saying a word. Everything good I try to do in this life, I do to make you proud. You're the strongest person I know, the hardest working person I know, and the foundation for anything I am or may ever be. Without you, I wouldn't be alive, much less writing a book, and even though that's obvious, I think it is worth saying. I appreciate the lessons and the strength you've given me through the years, but mostly for loving me in a way that no-one else can. I love you and appreciate you.

And to Blair, the first person who read this book back when it was a draft and when what we had was just a crush. It seems then that you saw the beauty in this book as I quietly saw the beauty in you. It shocking how quickly things can grow. It seems that even then before I truly knew you, you gave me something so personal that I couldn't help but love you for it. Life without you wasn't whole, and life with you is more than. Your love and support drive me to reach beyond the bounds of who I am.

Thank you for seeing and believing in me and what I do. You're my angel. You're my heart. I love you.

Enjoyed this Book?

Firstly, thank you so much for reading. If only I could personally express to each of you how much I appreciate you taking the time to buy and read these words. So many times, again and again, thank you.

Whether it be defending your opinion on social media or attempting to operate a succesful small business, the internet has made our world infinately competitive.

Because of this, your reviews on novels such as this one can have an infinately dramatic impact.

So if you liked *A Whistle on the Waves*...
LEAVE A REVIEW on Amazon or Goodreads.

Thank you so much.

The Trouble With Dead Terriers

The Shocking Dark Comedy Short and the First published work from K.M. Woods.

Amazon #1 New Release in Dark Humor

The once-wealthy marriage of Christoph and Desiree Wheeler crumbles into disarray when the family's teacup terrier, Bonnie, unexpectedly dies. Hidden secrets of betrayal reveal themselves as the Wheelers discover that this tiny, pampered animal may have been the glue holding them together for so long, and how harshly her unfortunate death may rip them apart.

Visit K.M. Woods at www.kmwoodsauthor.com
There you can purchase this book, find information on upcoming new works, sign up for my newsletter, or submit a poem to be read on the HOT WET POETRY CHANNEL.

www.ingramcontent.com/pod-product-compliance
Lightning Source LLC
Chambersburg PA
CBHW032023050726

47590CB00006B/2281